BE PRE

A TWISTED TALE NOVEL

FARRAH ROCHON

AUTUMN
PUBLISHING

AUTUMN
PUBLISHING

Published in 2025
First published in the UK by Autumn Publishing
An imprint of Igloo Books Ltd
Cottage Farm, NN6 0BJ, UK
Owned by Bonnier Books
Sveavägen 56, Stockholm, Sweden
www.igloobooks.com

0325 001
2 4 6 8 10 9 7 5 3 1
ISBN 978-1-83544-271-5

Cover illustrated by Giuseppe Di Maio

Printed and manufactured in the UK

BE PREPARED

A TWISTED TALE NOVEL

Dedicated to Brandon Michael. Tee Farrah
loves you more than words can describe.

– F.R.

PROLOGUE

Worn, brittle elephant tusks jutted from the earth, their pitted tips scratching at the sky like claws. A faint cloud of dust hovered in the air, adding to the creepiness of the abandoned Elephant Graveyard Nala and her best friend, Simba, had sneaked off to, well outside the boundary of the land where their pride of lions resided.

Trepidation rumbled in the pit of Nala's stomach, but she did her best to shield it from Simba. She was ahead in their ongoing game of one-upmanship, and she refused to cede the top spot to him. She had to be brave. Courageous. She could do this.

They inched closer to an enormous set of tusks, climbing up the crumbly side. Then they peered over them.

"Whoa," Nala and Simba whispered at the same time.

Giant thick elephant bones stretched as far as her eyes could see. There must have been a hundred of them – some piled on top of each other and even more scattered about the dry, desolate land.

"It's really creepy," Nala admitted.

"Yeah… isn't it great?" Simba said.

"We could get in big trouble," she cautioned.

"I know."

They climbed down from the tusks and ventured closer to the elephant skull, only to have Zazu, King Mufasa's pesky majordomo, intercept them. They should have expected this. Simba's dad often sent Zazu to accompany him, knowing that the king's son would be a target. The annoying red-billed hornbill prattled on about how far they were from the Pride Lands' boundary and the danger it posed. Nala had secretly felt the same way, but she had not wanted to say anything to Simba for fear he would scoff at her.

Or worse, call her a baby.

Simba was mocking Zazu in that brash, cocky way of his when maniacal cackling rang out from inside the elephant skull.

Hyenas!

How had she not smelt them coming? She could

usually detect their rank odour from a mile away.

Nala's bones quaked in fear as the mangy dogs slithered towards them, their sharp, yellowed fangs protruding from their mouths. For once she was grateful for Zazu, as he offered a layer of protection between her and Simba and those hyenas.

Zazu tried to guide them out of the Elephant Graveyard, but the hyenas blocked their escape at every turn. Nala's alarm escalated as she realised the threat they now faced. They had invaded the hyenas' land, which meant the hyenas could do whatever they wanted to them.

Simba tried to be brave, but Nala could sense his fear. He tried to use his position as the future king to reason with them, but the hyenas did not belong to their kingdom. It meant nothing to them.

Luck must have been on their side, though, because the hyenas started telling silly jokes, their attention on one another instead of Nala and Simba. Had they actually distracted themselves? What idiots.

Nala grabbed at the opportunity, catching Simba's eye and motioning behind them with her head. They took off, dodging rocks and skeletons as they sprinted across the graveyard.

"Did we lose them?" Nala panted, glancing over her shoulder.

"I think so," Simba said.

They paused for a moment and turned.

"Where's Zazu?" Simba asked.

Realising the hyenas must have captured him, Simba and Nala raced back to where they'd just left. They found the three mangy dogs standing around one of the natural geysers that littered this area. They were trying to stuff Zazu into the boiling water.

"Hey, why don't you pick on someone your own size?" Simba shouted.

"Like... you?" the leader of the hyena pack asked.

Great. Simba and his big mouth. When would he learn?

Just then, all three hyenas attacked, sending both Nala and Simba on another scramble. They dashed from one corner of the graveyard to another, doing all they could to outrun the hyenas. The slippery skeletal remains made it difficult to gain purchase as Nala tried to climb over them.

But their options ran out once they reached the towering wall of the gorge. It was too tall for either of them to scale. There was nowhere else to turn, no possible means of escape.

Simba blasted the hyenas with his mightiest growl, which Nala had to admit needed some work. It did nothing to deter the slobbering predators, who continued to advance.

Suddenly an earth-shattering roar shook the ground,

and Mufasa appeared from out of nowhere.

Saved by their king! Thank goodness.

Nala looked on in awe as Mufasa ravaged the hyenas. He took on all three with barely any effort, sending them scurrying back to the holes they'd crawled out of.

But when he finally faced Nala and Simba, Mufasa was the angriest Nala had ever seen him.

She knew that she and Simba should never have come here; knew they had tricked both of their mothers into believing they were going somewhere safe. She had also known that, if they were caught, there would be a price to pay. From the look of Mufasa's dark scowl, that price would be higher than she had anticipated.

They left the Elephant Graveyard in silence, nothing but a thick layer of tension pulsing in the air around them. They stopped when they were still a ways from home, surrounded by the tall grasslands just inside the perimeter of the kingdom.

At their king's command, Zazu and Nala began the journey back to Pride Rock. An ache settled in her throat at the thought of Simba having to face his father's wrath. She hated to leave him but was also grateful that she would not be subjected to the 'lesson' the king vowed to teach his son.

Mufasa's barely contained anger was a thing of nightmares, but it was the look of utter disappointment on his face that Nala knew she would never forget.

Three days later...

Nala huddled against her mother's paw, not wanting to believe the news Simba's uncle, Scar, had brought back to Pride Rock. He had just come from the gorge on the southern edge of the Pride Lands where the unthinkable had occurred. His words echoed around Nala's head like a jumbled mess that she could not process, no matter how much she tried.

A wildebeest stampede.

Mufasa. Dead.

Simba.

Dead.

Her friend – her *best* friend – was no longer here. Just the thought was too painful for her mind to comprehend. How could he be gone?

Simba had asked her to join him when he'd set out this morning, but Nala had been too afraid of upsetting her mother after their journey to the Elephant Graveyard a few days ago. She had begged him not to leave Pride Rock.

Why had she not been more forceful and demanded he stay? What if she could have saved him from this fate?

How could she have let her best friend down?

Nala looked around at the lionesses who all crowded together, comforting Sarabi. The sadness and shock on their faces mirrored what Nala felt inside. Their queen had just lost both her mate and her son. Their pride had lost their leader and the one who was to lead them into the future. In a matter of moments, everything had changed.

And Nala knew, from this point on, her life would never be the same.

CHAPTER ONE

Six Months Later...

The brisk wind blowing in from the north whipped the dry, gritty soil into a dust cloud, providing the perfect cover for Nala as she scoped out a hiding place. All was quiet except for the musical chirping of a family of magpies that flew overhead. She was close enough to Pride Rock to see it, but far enough to be barred from hearing the goings-on of the lionesses.

She took a step forwards, then quickly jerked back her paw, flattening herself against the boulder where she and Kamari, the lone boy cub of their pride, had been holed up.

"Nala," Kamari whispered anxiously. "What do you see?"

"Shhh." She silenced him. Then, in a low murmur, she said, "Follow me, on the count of three."

She tapped her paw against the packed earth. *One. Two.*

"Now," Nala said before darting from behind the boulder and scampering up the side of the barren rocks scattered at the base of the bluff. Kamari quickly surpassed her, his slightly larger paws affording him a steadier grip.

"Hurry, Nala," he called down to her. "Get up here before someone sees you."

"I'm trying," she hissed between her teeth.

Maybe if the trees that used to bloom around the Pride Lands still had leaves, it would be easier for Kamari and her to hide from the other cubs. But ever since Scar had taken over as king of the Pride Lands, nothing seemed to want to grow here. Their once-verdant lands were now arid, lifeless.

Nala could not blame the vegetation for remaining buried within the earth. Very little of this dry land appealed to her anymore either.

At least she still had her friends. Or at least *one* friend.

But could she really consider Kamari a friend? He was the only cub who would agree to partner with her during their game of Tig. But she was pretty sure he only did so because his mother made him.

Nala finally reached the flat top of the short bluff. She spotted Kamari's tail swishing on the other side of a crescent-shaped boulder and settled in opposite him. She crept to the edge of the overhang and peered out at the land. There weren't many places to hide; the drought of the last season had left much of the grasslands bare of their usual tall reeds.

"Do you see them?" Nala whispered to her partner.

"I see *you*."

Nala gasped and twisted around, her heart sinking at the sight of Ola.

"And now you're it," the older cub said, tapping Nala's hind leg with her paw.

Nala looked around, searching for Kamari. She saw him hightailing it across the parched ground, dust kicking up from underneath his paws.

So much for her trusty friend.

No fair. She shouldn't be tigged if her partner had bailed on her.

"I don't know why you even try to play this game," Ola said. "You're so bad at it."

Why did she play? Maybe because this was one of the few games her mother *allowed* her to play? It was the one game the other lion cubs engaged in that kept them close to Pride Rock and, thus, within minutes of her mother's reach.

"How am I supposed to get better at it if I don't practise?" Nala asked.

Ola scoffed, "We would have to play night and day for you to get any better. Come on, let's get going. You're it," Ola reminded her.

Nala trudged back down the side of the bluff and followed Ola to where the other cubs had gathered at the base of a jackalberry tree. Now that Kamari had run off, their numbers were uneven, leaving her without a partner.

"Uh… does anyone want to partner with me?" Nala asked. She already knew the answer even before several of the cubs stepped back. She swallowed past the pain suddenly lodged in her throat. It was one thing to sense you were a pariah amongst your pridemates, but another thing entirely to see them physically move away from you like you had a rash from having rolled around in asthma plant.

"I'll be your partner," a tinny voice squeaked. It was Abena, Ola's younger sister and the smallest cub of the entire pride. She raced up to Nala's side. "I can do it. I'm great at being invisible."

"Go back to the water hole," Ola said. "Mum told you that you're too young to play with us."

"Maybe Nala should join her," one of the other cubs said, "since her mummy thinks the same thing."

Several of the cubs snickered, and Nala felt the fur on the back of her neck stand up, but she remained silent. She was used to their teasing. Could she blame them?

Her mother *did* treat her as if she were Abena's age, a young cub incapable of making even the tiniest decision on her own.

"Thanks," Nala said to Abena, "but I can't play anymore. I hurt my paw climbing down from the rock."

"Yeah, right," Ola said. "Will that be your excuse tonight when we start the Hunting Games?"

That sinking feeling returned to Nala's chest.

The Hunting Games.

She had been dreading the kick-off of this annual rite of passage when the junior cubs of the pride were expected to showcase their skill at seeking out and executing a proper kill. The other cubs were eager to start; it was all any of them could talk about for the past week. But that's because *they* were prepared for it, unlike Nala.

For the last six months, most of the cubs in their pride had joined the lionesses on their nightly hunts, but Nala's mother, Sarafina, had refused to allow her to take part. She'd insisted it was too dangerous and that Nala would have time to learn how to hunt once she was older.

The thing her mother didn't seem to grasp was that Nala *was* getting older, and every day that passed without her practising how to hunt put her further behind in learning the most important skill any young cub needed to learn.

"Do you think we'll get to hunt an antelope?" Kamari's younger sister, Lindiwe, asked. "My mother taught me the perfect way to sneak up on them. First, you have to—"

"Don't share it with everyone," Bontu told her. "Save it for your team."

"What if you're not on my team?" Lindiwe asked.

"Then she loses," said Kahina, another of the cubs.

"No, the losers are whoever have Nala on their team," Ola said. All the cubs fell over laughing.

Nala wished she were near a sinkhole. She would dive right into it; anything to escape their unrelenting ridicule. She had forgotten that the junior cubs would be required to hunt in teams for this first night of the Hunting Games. It was bound to be another humiliating episode of watching every cub – even the younger ones – get picked before she did.

"It's not fair that a team has to get stuck with her," Kahina said, speaking about Nala as if she weren't standing right there.

"Does she even know how to pounce?" Lindiwe asked.

"Of course I know how to pounce," Nala said. It was the one skill she had learnt before…

Well, before everything had changed.

"The Hunting Games are about more than just pouncing," Ola said. "Have you ever caught an impala?"

Nala shook her head. Ola knew that Nala had never even had the chance to hunt an impala.

"A zebra? You *have* to have caught a zebra. They're slow."

"No," Nala said through gritted teeth.

"Huh." Ola stuck her nose in the air. "Well, I guess there's a first time for everything."

"I caught an impala *and* a zebra on our last hunt," Bontu said. "And I almost caught a gazelle too, but *some*one scared it away." She swished her tail at Lindiwe.

Nala stood back and listened as they regaled each other about the fun they'd had on their previous hunts, her heart twisting with every teasing laugh they shared. She'd tried to tell herself that she didn't care she didn't belong to their group, but she *did* care. This was her pride. Soon they would all grow into lionesses together, and she would be expected to hunt alongside them, to provide for the family.

What would happen to her when she could not pull her own weight? Would she be banished from the Pride Lands? How could she blame them if that was what they chose to do?

"Nala!" Nala's eyes fell closed at the sound of her mother's shrill, panicked voice. "Nala, where are you?"

The other cubs began to snicker again as they gave her a wide berth.

"Uh-oh, sounds like someone's in trouble for getting too far away from mummy," one of the cubs said.

Nala was about to respond, but her mother came upon them before she could utter another word.

"There you are," Sarafina said, rounding the jackalberry tree. Her breaths soughed in and out, as if she had been racing at breakneck speed. She placed her paw on Nala's head, her eyes roaming over her face as if looking for a blemish of some sort.

"What have I told you about wandering away?" Sarafina asked.

"I didn't wander away, Mum," Nala said. "And I'm with the other cubs. You told me I could play Tig. Remember?"

"I also told you that you had to remain where I could see you," Sarafina said. "I thought one of those awful hyenas had made away with you."

"Mum."

"Do not 'Mum' me." She placed a paw around Nala's shoulders. "The savanna is a dangerous place, Nala. Pride Rock isn't as safe as it once was. Ever since…" She paused. "Since… before."

She did not have to clarify what she meant by *before*. Everyone knew.

Before Mufasa and Simba met their untimely deaths.

Sarafina pulled Nala closer to her. She glanced at the cubs gathered around the tree, that haunted look Nala had come to know all too well clouding her eyes.

"The other lionesses may be okay with their cubs being out and about, but I won't have it," Sarafina said. "Now come with me. That's enough play time for today."

Nala was too embarrassed to look back at the other cubs as she walked tucked alongside her mother. As they made their way towards Pride Rock, Nala debated whether to broach the subject of the Hunting Games but knew she couldn't avoid it.

"Um, Mum, do you know what tonight is?"

"No, what?" Sarafina asked.

"It's the start of the Hunting Games."

"Oh, that," she said as if it were just any old night. "Yes, it is to begin shortly after sundown."

"What am I supposed to do?" Nala asked.

"What do you mean?"

"I will be expected to take part."

"Well, of course you will," Sarafina said. "Every young cub takes part in the Hunting Games."

Nala didn't think she should have to explain the obvious, but apparently she did. "How am I supposed to take part in the games, Mum? I don't know the first thing about hunting."

"Yes, you do. The first thing to hunting is knowing how to pounce, and I have seen you pounce before. You're very good at it."

"I've pounced on crickets," Nala pointed out. "And this isn't the *Pouncing* Games, it's the *Hunting* Games. I will be expected to hunt."

"You'll do fine," Sarafina said. "Just do your best. You're still a cub. No one expects you to take down a zebra."

But that was exactly what Nala and the other cubs would be expected to do. Tonight was their initiation into the practice of stalking prey and providing sustenance for their pride. There was not a lion in the entire savanna who would be satisfied with a diet of crickets or other bugs.

"Mum, you don't seem to understand—"

"Nala, you will do just fine," her mother said, cutting her off. "Now come. It's time for a bath. You don't want to show up to the Hunting Games with dirty ears."

Yeah, because *that* was the important thing here.

As much as Nala wished it were not the case, there was no avoiding the heartbreaking truth: tonight would be a disaster.

CHAPTER TWO

A sense of excitement saturated the air as the pride readied itself for this much-anticipated celebration of its youth. Crisscrossed gazelle horns marked the two spots where the opposing teams were to gather, but for now the six cubs participating in tonight's games stood in a wide circle in the shadow of Pride Rock.

Dusk had just settled over the land, the melodious calls of the crickets, cicadas and grasshoppers ringing through the clearing as the insects ventured out. The full moon shone bright in the sky, illuminating the members of their pride assembled for the evening.

Four of the twelve fully grown lionesses that made up their pride had been dispatched to the southern edge of the

Pride Lands, where a pack of wild hogs had been seen earlier in the day. They would be doing the *real* hunting tonight. At one time the lionesses could hunt every three or four days and provide enough food for them all to subsist on, but ever since the hyenas had moved onto their lands – at their new king's invitation, no less – lionesses were forced to hunt every single night to keep up with the hyenas' ravenous appetites.

It was yet another reason why this year's Hunting Games felt so intense. They needed hunters now more than ever.

And it was why Nala already felt like a failure to her pride.

Her stomach roiled as she waited for the ceremony to begin. She shivered despite the warmth of the breeze that blew across the Pride Lands.

She looked up at the sky, towards the cluster of stars she had deemed Simba's.

Just before he perished, her friend had told her about a conversation he'd had with Mufasa, about how the kings of the past looked down on them from the stars. Nala had spent so many nights staring up at the sky over these past six months, willing herself to feel *something*. All she needed was a sign, some indication that Simba was up there. That he was looking out for her, cheering for her. If there was ever a time she needed a sign that her friend had her back, it was tonight.

But it would take more than wishing on stars to save her from utter humiliation. It would take a miracle.

Stop that! Nala mentally chastised.

She was probably putting too much pressure on herself. No one expected her to be perfect. Perfection wasn't expected of any of the cubs. Tonight's kill – if they were lucky enough to make one – would provide sustenance, but the pride was not counting on the cubs' skills for survival.

At least not yet.

They all waited for Sarabi to make her grand entrance, as was tradition. Even though her life mate no longer ruled as king, no one disputed that Sarabi remained the queen of their kingdom. All the lionesses deferred to her.

Nala's breath caught in her throat as she watched Simba's mother make her way to them, her regal head held high. The lionesses and cubs all bowed as she marched towards them with measured steps, her journey ending in the centre of the circle.

"Welcome to the time-honoured tradition of the Hunting Games," Sarabi began. She slowly walked around the circle, staring each cub in the eye. "Our pride has ruled this kingdom for generations, in large part thanks to our skilled lionesses. There is no equal in all the savanna. Tonight the newest class of hunters will display what they have learnt."

Or not learnt.

Disaster. Disaster. Disaster.

The word rattled around in Nala's head like a tumbleweed blowing across the dusty savanna.

"You have been preparing for this since shortly after your birth, and the preparation will continue long after this night has passed. But you have reached a point where it is time to assess where you stand in your tutelage." Sarabi stepped to the side. "Thandi will now explain the rules of tonight's games."

The lioness, who Nala learnt had participated in the games during the same season her own mother had, entered the circle and began to lay out instructions for tonight's activities.

"Cubs will be randomly selected to join one of two teams," Thandi said.

Randomly selected?

Nala was so relieved that she would be spared the embarrassment of having to stand here while her fellow cubs picked everyone *but* her to be on their team that she could have cried.

And yet, it turned out that it was just as humiliating to be randomly placed on teams as it would have been if the cubs had picked themselves. Her name was the fifth called, and her two teammates, Bontu and the always quiet Puleng – who was even younger than Nala – both groaned when

Nala was ordered to stand with them in front of the gazelle horns.

Her heart sank even further into the pit of her stomach when she glanced over and caught the look shared between Lindiwe's and Kahina's mothers. The two lionesses seemed to be quietly celebrating the fact that their daughters had not been saddled with Sarafina's disappointing cub.

Ola, Lindiwe and Kahina now stood across from them with matching grins as if they already knew they would be crowned victors.

Nala sent a silent prayer up to the ancestors asking to be instantly blessed with hunting skills so that she could wipe the smug look off their competitors' faces.

"Don't mess this up," Bontu hissed at Nala.

She wanted to tell her that she wouldn't, but the likelihood that she would make a spectacular fool of herself in front of everyone was much too high.

"I'll try not to," Nala answered. "I'm sorry."

It wasn't their fault she was not prepared for tonight. It wasn't her fault either.

She looked to her mother, who smiled and nodded. Nala could not summon a return smile. It took all she had within her not to lash out.

This was her mother's doing. She was the one who refused to let Nala practise her hunting with the other cubs.

She was the one who quickly snatched Nala back whenever she got too far away from her side.

Ever since Simba's death, her mother had become obsessed with keeping Nala safe. She panicked if she went too long without putting her eyes on Nala, and when it came to Nala's doing anything she deemed dangerous – which, these days, was as simple as Nala's going to the water hole with fellow cubs – Sarafina was quick to shoot it down.

She was so afraid of something happening to Nala that she treated her as if she were a brand-new baby cub, born hours ago.

And tonight Nala would be made to suffer the consequences of her mother's irrational fear.

Thandi stepped back so that Sarabi, moving to the middle of the two teams, could reclaim her spot.

"The time has come for our junior cubs to make us proud," Sarabi said. "Let the Hunting Games begin!"

Bontu and Puleng darted for the brush that was just west of the water hole, where small fowl and rodents tended to live, while the other team went in the opposite direction, towards the embankment where Nala and Kamari had hidden during their game of Tig.

"Come on, Nala, follow close behind," Puleng called in a loud whisper. "Remember, don't make a sound."

She was making a sound. She was making *many* sounds.

And it wasn't as if she needed Puleng's instructions. She may not have had much practice in hunting, but she knew the basics.

"I know that," Nala answered.

"Shhh," Bontu chastised.

She wanted to point out that Puleng had made way more noise than she had, but all she would gain from that was another rebuke. Instead Nala concentrated on listening for prey.

She closed her eyes and slowed her breaths. Some things were taught, but others were instinctual, like that sense you got when you weren't alone. She couldn't explain it; she could only *feel* it.

Nala heard the faint sound of rustling reeds near the edge of the water. Something was there. A gazelle? An antelope? How amazing would it be if she captured an antelope!

She glanced over at her teammates. They were looking in the opposite direction.

This was her chance.

If she was going to prove to her fellow cubs that she was not a total loser, this was the time to do it.

Nala called on the memories of the pouncing lessons she'd had with Simba, staying low and stalking her prey in a slow and calculated manner. Inch by inch, she crept towards the water, doing her best to keep her tail motionless. One swish could send the grass rustling and her potential catch scurrying.

She peered through the reeds and spotted a tiny bat-eared fox. It was no antelope, but it would count as a kill. She took three delicate steps forwards. Then, with a burst of speed, she took off for the fox. She pounced on it, but before she could clamp down on its neck, it shrugged loose of her grip and took off.

"Nala!"

She whipped around to find Puleng and Bontu approaching.

"How did you let that fox get away?" Puleng asked.

"I tried to catch it," Nala complained. She motioned to the cub's empty paws. "At least I had something in my sights. What did either of *you* catch?"

"Shhh," Puleng said, dipping low.

Nala glanced around quickly before dropping to the ground. She watched as Puleng glided through the weeds. Before Nala could spot what she hunted, the cub shot forwards and in seconds came back with the same fox that had escaped from Nala's grasp.

Puleng dropped its lifeless body on the ground in front of Nala and said, "*This* is what I caught."

"And we could have had a warthog if you hadn't made

so much noise trying to catch this little baby fox," Bontu said. "We were going to double-team him, but now he's run off."

"The first lesson in hunting is to not scare off the prey," Puleng said.

"You're useless," Bontu told her.

Nala wanted to argue, but how could she blame them for being upset? She would be upset too if she were in their position. The other cubs had worked hard preparing for this night, and she was letting them down.

"I'm sorry" was all she could say.

"Yeah, you are," Bontu said. She rolled her eyes. "Let's go further west. Maybe we can spot a baby wildebeest that's fallen behind in the migration."

Nala hesitated. Her mother would have a fit if she travelled much further from Pride Rock. Just south of the water hole was the furthest she had journeyed in six months. If she couldn't see the tip of Pride Rock, she knew she had gone too far.

But tonight's circumstances were different. There was no way her mother expected her to stay within her usual boundaries during the Hunting Games.

"Nala, come on," Puleng called from several paces ahead of her.

Nala looked back over her shoulder before sprinting

to catch up with her team. They had just passed the thick baobab tree that marked where the grasslands met the scrubland when Nala heard her name being called.

Or, more accurately, shrieked.

Not again.

"What is that?" Puleng asked.

"Nala! Nala, answer me now," she heard her mother yell.

"Sarafina, she is fine. Let her be," a second voice called. It sounded like Sefu, another of the lionesses. "It's the Hunting Games, for goodness' sake!"

"I don't care! Nala!"

Puleng and Bontu both stared at her with furious scowls. Nala was too mortified to speak. She stood frozen, her limbs rigid with embarrassment.

"Nala!" Her mother's cry sounded desperate.

"We're over here," Bontu called out, her eyes still trained on Nala.

"I'm sorry," Nala whispered past the lump of humiliation lodged in her throat.

"You're such a baby," Puleng spat. "I knew this would happen if you were on our team."

Sarafina arrived, followed quickly by Sefu.

"There you are. Thank goodness," her mother said. She wrapped her paws around Nala and gave her head a deep lick. Then she reared back and, in a stern voice, said, "You know better than to wander this far. What were you thinking?"

"I wasn't wandering," Nala argued. "And it's not as if I was alone. I have my team with me."

"You're all cubs!" Sarafina said. "What if a cougar, or hyenas, or a lion from another pride came around? Do you think you and your team would be able to fend them off?"

"Sarafina, you know there are lionesses stationed throughout the Pride Lands tonight," Sefu said. "No harm is going to come to any of the cubs."

"You don't know that," her mother said.

"We take special precautions during the Hunting Games. You *know* this."

"I don't care. I'm pulling Nala out of the games. She can participate next time."

"Mum, no," Nala said.

"My decision is final," her mother said. "Follow me back to Pride Rock."

A feeling of hopelessness washed over her. If her mother refused to allow her to participate in something as important to their pride as the Hunting Games, when would Sarafina ever loosen this grip she had on her?

Nala lowered her head. With a heavy sigh, she began walking behind her mother.

"So, what does this mean for the games?" Nala heard Bontu ask.

"I don't know," Sefu answered. "It isn't fair to have a team with just two members. I shall ask Sarabi what she wants to do about the continuation of the games."

Several other lionesses met Nala and Sarafina when they were still some distance from Pride Rock. They questioned what had happened, but Sarafina refused to answer them. When Sarabi asked upon their return, Sarafina simply said that Nala was not suited for the games this year.

Everyone knew *that* well before the start of tonight's ceremony. Why had her mother allowed her to participate at all? If she had told her no from the beginning, then she would have at least spared Nala the embarrassment of being chased down like a baby cub who had wandered too far from home.

Sefu, Bontu and Puleng arrived shortly after Nala and her mother had returned, and Sefu provided the explanation that everyone sought.

Nala caught the frustrated glance Sarabi directed at Sarafina, but her mother's attention was on something in the distance. Nala looked in the direction she was staring, and her stomach plummeted as she saw the other team dragging a black-and-white-striped carcass towards Pride Rock.

"A zebra! They captured a zebra!" cheered Fayola, Ola and Abena's mother.

Bontu and Puleng both stared Nala down with matching infuriated looks while a group of lionesses raced out to help the other team haul in their kill. Ola, Lindiwe and Kahina were showered with praise as the pride celebrated their victory.

This had turned out to be even worse than Nala had first imagined, and she had imagined it would be pretty awful.

She slipped away, just outside the circle of lionesses. She could not stomach seeing the success of the other team, knowing that *she* was the reason her own hadn't achieved the same.

Nala lay on her stomach and rested her chin on her paws. Even though she had been in this same position – on the outside looking in, wishing she could be part of the group – countless times since Simba left her, she had never felt so disconnected from her own pride as she did in that very moment. Disconnected and alone.

Nala scrambled up from the ground and narrowed her eyes as she tracked Ola and Kahina sauntering towards her.

"Con— congratulations," she told them. They were, after all, the victors.

"Thanks," Ola said. "So… what did your team kill?"

"We…" Nala swallowed. "Puleng killed a fox."

"One fox? That's all? Not even an aardvark? Even Abena can catch an aardvark."

"No aardvarks, only the fox," Bontu said as she stepped up to them. "Her mummy made her come back to Pride Rock before we even got to the scrubland. All of us had to come back because of her."

Ola and Kahina burst out laughing.

"I am so glad you weren't on our team," Ola said. She huffed and stared down her nose at Nala. "You thought you were such hot stuff back when you got to spend all day playing with the future king. Now look at you."

Nala flinched at her words.

"She was only friends with Simba because Sarabi and Sarafina are best friends," Kahina said.

"That's not true," Nala whispered. Every horrible thing they said felt like sharp claws lashing her cheek.

"Yes, it is," Ola said. "Face it, Nala. Without Simba, you're nothing around here."

Nala felt the tears welling in her eyes but refused to let them fall while the other cubs were around. She needed to get away before she made an even bigger fool of herself.

And there was only one place she wanted to be right now. Only one place she *could* be.

She pushed past Ola and the others and raced to Pride Rock.

CHAPTER THREE

"What is that ruckus?"

Scar draped his body across the smooth boulder in his sleeping quarters and tried to tune out the noise coming from somewhere near Pride Rock. Didn't these lionesses realise he'd only had fifteen hours of sleep today? How was he supposed to function as their king if he was too tired to even think?

"It is the Hunting Games, Sire," Zazu, his majordomo, answered.

Scar eyed the bird suspiciously. He was never sure if the annoying little fowl was telling him the truth or not, so he never took anything Zazu said at face value.

If there was one thing Scar wasn't, it was an idiot.

He knew Zazu was still loyal to Mufasa. Which meant Zazu was not to be fully trusted, no matter how much he tried to placate him.

Scar could feel his mane at the back of his neck standing at attention. It happened whenever his brother crossed his mind, which was far too often. How silly of him to think ridding this world of Mufasa would be the end of his trouble. It seemed as if things had only become more dire since Mufasa's untimely demise.

Untimely, but still necessary.

"Remind me again, what are the Hunting Games?" Scar asked.

"Oh, you know," Zazu said. "It is when the cubs get to show off their hunting skills. It happens whenever a new class of lionesses comes of age."

"Well, do they have to be so loud? I thought the lionesses were supposed to remain quiet when they stalked their prey."

"There must be a victor already, if the sounds of the celebration are anything to go on," Zazu said. "I wonder which group of cubs won."

As if that mattered.

Scar rolled off the boulder and slunk out of the cave. The dry season had lasted much longer than it had in years past – something everyone had taken note of – but there was a weight to the air tonight, an indication that the torrential rains of their wet season would soon be upon them.

He walked to the ledge that protruded from Pride Rock so that he could peer out onto the Pride Lands. He caught sight of the lionesses, and those hairs on the back of his neck flexed again.

Half the pride – many of the fully grown lionesses and most of the cubs – was gathered in the clearing between Pride Rock and the water hole. He couldn't tell the little ones apart yet, not that he had ever tried. Who had time to learn all those names?

Even from this distance, Scar could make out the zebra carcass that lay on the ground. His mouth immediately began to water. A zebra leg would be the most amazing bedtime snack.

Maybe he could put up with their noise if it meant the cubs would bring in more food. An antelope lasted less than a day around these parts now that the hyenas shared their home. Those greedy mutts ate everything in sight.

Scar emitted a growl at the thought of the hyenas.

They were a nuisance, but at least they showed him respect. Which was more than he could say for his own pride.

The lionesses would eventually come around. He would find a way to gain the respect of each and every one of them.

He had no choice, and neither did they.

Although, as he had unfortunately discovered over these last six months, there was no way to bully them into respecting him as their leader. Oh, they deferred to him – he *was* their king, after all, and the laws of their kingdom must be followed – but they did so with disgust in their eyes.

If they chose to look at him at all.

What made it so much harder to swallow was the knowledge that, were Mufasa still here, there would be no question of where their loyalty resided. Scar knew what he needed to do; he just was unsure how to go about it. How was he supposed to shed his rather questionable past if the lionesses wouldn't give him the chance?

Maybe if he showed more interest in them? Like learning the names of their cubs?

He slouched against a rock.

Goodness, just the thought made him want to hurl his dinner. But if pretending that he cared about more than merely the food the lionesses provided for him and his friends would gain him some respect, then that was what he must do.

Well, at least he had his dodo bird to do his bidding.

"Zazu," Scar called.

He waited an entire minute before the bird finally

heeded his call. It irritated him. If it were Mufasa who had summoned him, this little sack of feathers would have been at his side in seconds.

"Yes, Sire," Zazu said.

Scar stared down his nose at him for several moments, letting him know without words that he was unhappy with the lack of promptness.

"Forgive my tardiness, Sire," Zazu said.

Scar acknowledged his apology with a curt nod, then he gestured with his head towards the clearing.

"I want you to go down there and gather information for me. Find out which of the cubs won their little... game. Let them know that I applaud their work."

"Well, Sire, if you don't mind my saying, maybe it would be better if you were to do it yourself. Then they can witness your approval first-paw."

Scar had thought of that but quickly dismissed it. He had served as the pride leader long enough to know how the lionesses would react to his presence. The tone of the festivities would change the moment he appeared. Or they would end altogether, the same way the lionesses all stopped talking whenever he came around.

No, he would rather send Zazu. They trusted the little bird. He would go so far as to say they liked him, though Scar had no idea why. Zazu was a pain.

But he was useful.

"No, you should go," Scar told him. "Sarabi, for one, will be happy to see you."

Scar purposely limited the time Zazu spent with all the lionesses, but especially with his brother's widow. He didn't want the two of them putting their heads together and coming up with some sort of plan to oust him from the throne.

But happy lionesses made for better hunters, so it was best to keep them as happy as possible. And maybe, if they were happy, then they would finally start to come around.

He looked back at Zazu and said, "Go."

CHAPTER FOUR

Nala gingerly made her way across the collection of gritty stones, on her way to her favourite… no, she could not call it her favourite place. Not anymore. But it was her most sacred place in the entire savanna, the place she felt most at ease.

She continued to wind her way up the back side of Pride Rock, climbing over rocks and boulders that had become easier to scale as she had grown older. Maybe by the time she was a fully grown lioness she would be able to reach her special place in no time at all. She came upon the two-foot-wide crevice that marked the midway point and gave herself a running start before leaping across it.

She was halfway to her destination when she rounded

another boulder… and screamed.

"Oh, oh! Miss Nala!" Zazu cawed, flapping his colourful wings.

"Zazu!" Nala leaned back against the boulder, her heart beating within her chest like antelope stomping across the Serengeti. "What are you doing here?"

"I should be asking the same of you," the bird said. "It's the Hunting Games. Why aren't you celebrating with the others?"

She rolled her eyes. "Well, there isn't much to celebrate when you're on the losing team," she said.

"Oh, fiddle-faddle. Everyone knows there are no real losers when it comes to the Hunting Games. All cubs will eventually learn to hunt, so you will win, no matter what. Come now, join me in the clearing."

"No," Nala said. "I just… I want to be alone."

Zazu peered down his beak at her, then nodded. "I understand," he said. "I guess tonight isn't quite what it would have been if… well, if Simba were here."

Nala sniffed. She would not cry in front of Zazu – or in front of anyone.

"Go on, then," he said. "I shall not disturb you."

With that, he took off, swooping around the boulder and continuing his flight down to where the others still gathered, their gleeful cheers piercing the quiet night.

Nala continued her climb up to her secret spot.

An instant sweeping sense of calm washed over her the moment she reached the pinnacle and spotted the smooth stone where she and Simba would watch the sunset. Nala moved cautiously towards it as if any sudden movement would disturb the memories that were etched into every part.

The sun had gone to bed hours ago, but the full moon cast its light over a good amount of the Pride Lands. It had been a long time since she had made it up to this secluded area of Pride Rock, but on a night like tonight she needed the peace this particular space brought her.

She needed to feel close to Simba.

She closed her eyes and summoned the memory of her very best friend.

"Oh, Simba," Nala whispered. "How I wish you were here."

She tried not to think about him these days because it just hurt too much, knowing he wouldn't answer if she called for him. She imagined how differently tonight would have played out had he been there. No way Ola or Kahina would have said the things they had said to her.

Because they would not have had cause to say any of it. Because if her best friend were here, Nala had no doubt that she would be able to hunt just as well as any of the other cubs. Probably even better.

Everything that had gone wrong in her life – the hurt, the pain, her mother's overbearing behaviour – stemmed from Simba's and Mufasa's deaths.

If Simba were still alive, her mother would not have turned into the overprotective lioness she had become. Nala would be allowed to scamper off into the scrubland, pouncing on unsuspecting hares and foxes and doing the things a normal cub her age was allowed to do.

Simba's death had changed it all.

"Why did you have to go?" Nala whispered.

She looked around, recalling them playing games of hide-and-seek and talking about all the things they would do when they were fully grown. She grinned as she thought about Simba's cocky answer to just about everything.

I can do this, because I'm going to be king.

But he would never be king.

Unless…

Nala shook her head, doing her best to toss out the thoughts that had invaded her mind, unbidden yet persuasive. Tonight was difficult enough; she did not need to start obsessing over the unfounded rumours that crept up from time to time. Simba would never be king because Simba was gone. Forever.

She knew this, yet a large part of her heart still held out hope.

The rumours that he wasn't dead, that he instead had

escaped the stampede that had taken Mufasa from them, had started soon after Scar had returned with the heartbreaking news of what had happened in the gorge. Every so often they would hear whispers of a Simba sighting. He'd been spotted with a family of giraffes in Mikumi or crossing the Great Ruaha River near Dodoma. But Nala knew better than to believe that. Simba would never head south.

Due to her mother's insistence that she remain close to her at all times, and her mother's friendship with Sarabi, Nala knew of Sarabi's network of animals throughout the savanna that were tasked with looking for him. But whenever one of them brought back a promising lead, another would soon return with a report dispelling the news.

Because there was no news. He was gone. Maybe if she finally accepted that – *truly* accepted it – life would get easier for her.

Nala looked around again. Everything her gaze fell upon was another memory. Sometimes she wished she could leave Pride Rock so that she didn't have to deal with all these reminders. And yet, the memories were all she had of Simba. If she left, she wouldn't have anything.

Besides, this was her home. It was her mother's home and had been the home of her grandmother. She could not imagine living any place but Pride Rock.

Even when she and Simba had bandied about their

dreams of taking off and seeing parts of the savanna and jungle that reached beyond the horizon, there was the knowledge that this place would always be here to welcome them back.

A thought occurred to her. What if she could live out some of those dreams she'd shared with Simba? Maybe then she would not feel so out of sorts.

"How are you going to do that?" Nala said with a snort. "You can't even go past the water hole."

And that was where her problem lay.

Nothing would ever be okay if she was forced to continue living under her mother's oppressive paw. If tonight had not shown her mum just how harmful her extreme overprotectiveness was to Nala's development, then nothing would.

Of course her mother *didn't* see it. She had pulled Nala from the Hunting Games without giving a thought to what such an act would mean in the long run.

But Nala knew what it meant, and the thought terrified her.

Her mother would not be here forever. Nala would eventually have to learn to hunt. If she didn't…

She'd heard stories of what happened to lionesses who were not willing or able to pull their own weight around the pride. They were exiled. Or worse.

Nala wouldn't have imagined her fellow cubs doing such a thing to her.

Until tonight.

Bontu's and Puleng's frustration with her lack of hunting skills, and their vitriol when Sarafina put a halt to the game, was an eye-opener. She had been subjected to Ola's and Kahina's relentless teasing for months, but they had taken it to another level after their win. Witnessing the way the other cubs had treated her tonight, Nala feared she was at risk of being banished from Pride Rock once they all reached full-grown status.

Someway, somehow, she would have to get through to her mother. Sarafina needed to realise that the more she shielded Nala, the more she was holding her back. And if things did not change soon, Nala would be the one who would be forced to pay.

She stood up, an idea coming to her as if something – or someone – had placed it directly into her mind.

Nala suddenly realised what she must do. She would get Sarabi to talk to her mother on her behalf.

She had noticed the way Sarabi had looked at her mother tonight upon their return from the scrubland. Nala was certain that a number of their pridemates had taken note of her mother's bizarre behaviour these last six months. She was pretty sure Sefu had tried to bring it up with her, but Sarabi was the only one her mother would truly listen to.

At least Nala hoped she would.

She climbed down from her and Simba's rock and started for the path back down Pride Rock, but then she halted her steps at the sight of a shadow projected onto a boulder. A moment later, a cub emerged.

"Puleng?" Nala asked.

The cub took several more steps forwards, her entire body now illuminated by the moonlight.

"Yes, it's me," Puleng answered. "I figured I would find you here when I didn't see you down in the clearing."

"But... how did you know where to look?"

Puleng tilted her head to the side. "Really, Nala? Everyone knows you come here when you want to be alone."

Nala wondered if everyone knew *why* she came here. Puleng answered before she could voice the question.

"I understand why," the cub said. "You and Simba used to come here all the time. We could sometimes see the tips of your heads from down below."

Nala's mouth fell open. She'd had no idea.

For some reason, the revelation disturbed her. She'd always thought of this place as her secret getaway, the place where she could escape to feel close to her friend. The only one who Nala thought had knowledge of it was her mother, and only because she had forced Nala to tell her.

Once she'd realised that Nala's little escape was on Pride Rock, she had no problem with her venturing up here alone.

But knowing that others knew about it, that they could even see her, tainted it.

"Did you need something?" Nala asked Puleng, still hurt from the cub's earlier treatment of her. She had at one time considered Puleng a friend.

"Yes," the cub said, averting her eyes. "I… umm… wanted to apologise for the things I said earlier during the Hunting Games. I was insensitive. Actually, I was pretty mean to you, and it was wrong."

Nala sucked in a swift breath. She had not been prepared for her own reaction to Puleng's words. She suddenly felt the same as when she lay huddled against her mother's side. Despite everything, there was still nothing more comforting than her mother's warmth.

"I really am sorry," Puleng said. She closed the distance between them. "I know that you *want* to learn how to hunt, Nala, and that it isn't your fault you've fallen so far behind the rest of us. I wish I could change it, or at least help you in some way. It didn't help that I was piling it on when Ola and the others had already been so ugly to you."

No, that had not helped, but hearing Puleng's apology did.

"Thank you for that," Nala said. It felt good to know that

she still had allies amongst the pride's cubs. "Let's go back to the celebration," Nala said. "I have something in mind that may encourage my mum to let me hunt."

"Really?" Puleng asked, her eyes bright with excitement.

"I hope so," Nala said. "Let's go."

And the two took off down the southern side of Pride Rock.

CHAPTER FIVE

Sarabi placed a crown fashioned out of braided lemongrass over Ola's head.

She was not happy with the young cub's brashness during tonight's Hunting Games – the way she'd lauded her team's win over the losing team's head was unbecoming of a lioness of their pride. She would speak with Fayola about her daughter's lack of graciousness. Although the communal nature of their pride allowed for all the lionesses to have a say in what went on with the cubs, there were some things that were the responsibility of the mother. This was one of those instances.

Still, the young cub *had* led the winning team. She had earned her place of honour in tonight's festivities.

"Congratulations," Sarabi told her. She couldn't help adding, "May you *humbly* accept this token of your pride's admiration."

"Next time I'll catch an even bigger zebra. I won't even need my teammates' help."

"Do you know what *humbly* means, Ola?" Sarabi asked.

Just then, Ola's younger sister, Abena, ran up to them.

"Let me wear it! Let me wear it!" she said, reaching for Ola's crown.

"No. Get away," Ola said, shaking her off. She darted towards the area where the other cubs had gathered, the much slower Abena trailing behind.

Sarabi stared at the retreating cubs and had to fight the pang of longing that nearly overwhelmed her.

She released an even deeper sigh when she spotted Nala standing underneath the bare branches of a bush willow. Sarabi waited for the familiar twinge to pierce her chest at the sight of the young cub. It was not as pronounced, but it was still there.

She had become so used to seeing Nala and Simba together that, to this day, she could not lay eyes on her son's closest pridemate without thinking of him. The fissure in Sarabi's heart widened a little more as she caught the sadness lurking in Nala's eyes. And she was pretty sure she knew the source of it.

Sarabi had yet to get the full story from Sefu, but she sensed she already had a good idea of what had occurred after the two lionesses took off for the water hole. She could only imagine the scene Sarafina had caused, racing after Nala, pulling her out of the games.

How could she have done such a thing? And in front of the cub's pridemates.

When Nala moved away from the bush willow, Sarabi figured the cub was heading to the spot in the clearing where the other cubs who had participated in tonight's games had all gathered. She flicked her head back in surprise when she realised Nala was instead walking directly towards *her*.

"Well, hello, Nala," Sarabi greeted. "How are you?"

Nala shrugged.

"If I'm being honest, I must say that you look a bit down."

"A little," Nala muttered.

"I hope it isn't because of the outcome of the Hunting Games. There is always a winning team and a losing team. That's just the way things are."

"I know," she said.

Sarabi leaned in closer to her ear. "Do you want to hear a secret?"

Nala looked up at her and nodded, her eyes wide.

"Well, it isn't so much a secret. It's just that there

are few still residing on Pride Rock who are old enough to remember. But back when I participated in my first Hunting Games, not only was my team on the losing end, but we failed to bring in a single kill."

"Not even a hare?" Nala asked.

"Not even a tiny little hare," Sarabi confirmed. "So, you see, you have nothing to be ashamed of. You, Bontu and Puleng all did us very proud tonight. And you will have the opportunity to participate in another Hunting Games before you reach full-grown status."

"That's just it," Nala said. She drew her paw in a slow circle on the ground, making grooves in the loose dirt. "The same thing will probably happen the next time."

"You don't know that—"

"Yes, I do," Nala said, a shade of desperation entering her voice. "How will anything change if I don't learn to hunt?"

"You will eventually learn to hunt, Nala."

She shook her head. "No, I won't. Not with the way my mother has been acting." Nala looked up at her, her eyes drowning in hurt. "She won't let me do anything, Sarabi. She barely allows me to play games with the other cubs. If I take just a few steps away from her, she's screaming for me to get back."

She did not have to explain. Sarabi had witnessed it

with her own eyes. All the lionesses had seen it. A few of them had even met to discuss what to do about Sarafina and her increasingly alarming overprotectiveness. The other lionesses had been gracious enough not to bring up what had triggered Sarafina's behaviour, but they all knew the catalyst behind it. It was the one reason why Sarabi had held off discussing it with her friend.

She had hoped it would get better in time, but the opposite had happened. Sarafina's smothering had become even more egregious.

"Will you talk to her?" Nala now asked.

Sarabi reared back. "Oh, Nala, I don't know."

"You *have* to," the cub pleaded. "You're the only one here who she will listen to. Sarabi, do you know what happens to full-grown lionesses who never learn to hunt?"

"Nothing will happen to you," Sarabi reassured her. "You belong to a pride that takes care of its own, no matter what."

"Prides change," Nala said. "You, my mother, Sefu and the others – you all will not live forever. It is something I did not think about very much before…" She let her words trail off.

"Oh, Nala," Sarabi whispered, reaching for her.

Nala jerked out of her reach. "But bad things happen," she continued. "It is not always bad things, it is just… life.

No lion lives forever. And when you and my mother and the other senior lionesses are gone, Ola and Kahina will be the lionesses running this pride. Something tells me they will not feel the same way about taking care of their own as you do."

Sarabi wanted to refute her words, to tell her she was worrying about issues that would never come to pass, but Nala had a point. Sarabi did not know what would become of this pride once she was no longer here. She hated the thought of Fayola's bossy cub controlling the Pride Lands but even if Sarabi were to anoint the next leader of their pride, Ola could always call for a challenge.

Sarabi closed her eyes, unable to bear the thought of the in-pride fighting that could ensue. It was the type of thing that could lead to the downfall of the Pride Lands.

"I need to learn how to hunt," Nala said. "I don't want to have to rely on my pridemates to hunt for me. I want to be able to contribute. And there is no reason that I should not learn to hunt, except that my mother thinks it is too dangerous. If it isn't too dangerous for Puleng, who is younger than I am, then it isn't too dangerous for me. My mum is not being reasonable."

Sarabi couldn't argue with her. It was not a question that Sarafina's irrational fears were holding Nala back, but it wasn't until the young cub had laid it out so succinctly that

Sarabi realised the true harm Sarafina was inadvertently causing her cub. She was leaving her ill-prepared to face the world, and in the end, it could put Nala in real danger.

"Okay," Sarabi said.

Nala's eyes widened. "Okay? You mean you'll do it? You'll talk to her?"

"Yes," Sarabi answered.

"When?"

She released a weighty sigh. "I guess there is no better time to do it than right now."

If she had considered backing down on her promise, the excited gratitude on Nala's face sealed her fate.

She led the way, with Nala following closely behind. They found Sarafina lounging near the trunk of a downed jackalberry tree with several of the other lionesses.

"Uh, Sarafina, can I speak with you? Over there?" Sarabi asked, gesturing towards Pride Rock with her head.

Sarafina tilted her head to the side, her eyebrows angling downwards with her confused frown.

"Is... is something wrong?" she asked, looking at Sarabi and then at Nala.

"Over there," Sarabi repeated. She motioned for Nala to stay back. This would probably be easier if Sarafina did not have the cause for her overprotective behaviour by her side.

"What is it?" her friend asked as soon as they'd arrived under the canopy created by the rock formation's protruding ledge.

"Sefu told me what happened tonight down at the scrubland," Sarabi opened.

"What is there to tell?" Sarafina asked, her tone becoming immediately defensive. "That I saved my daughter from almost certain danger?"

"Not a single cub was in any danger tonight. You have been around for enough Hunting Games to know that."

She huffed. "You sound just like Sefu."

"Because Sefu sees that you are getting out of paw with—"

"I don't care what any of you think," Sarafina shouted. "I have to protect Nala. She is all I have."

"I know that," Sarabi said. "But there is a fine line between protecting her and doing irreparable harm. Nala must learn to hunt."

"She will learn to—"

"When?" Sarabi asked, cutting *her* off this time. "Whenever the lionesses take the junior cubs out on a hunting expedition, you come up with an excuse for Nala to remain at Pride Rock. She will never learn the skills she needs to survive if you won't allow her to go past the water hole."

"Did she put you up to this?" Sarafina asked, pointing a paw at Nala. "Did you arrange this?" she called out to her daughter.

"Sarafina, don't," Sarabi said, reaching for her. But Sarafina shook her off, pulling out of her grasp and marching back towards where the others were gathered.

Sarabi ran after her. By the time she caught up with Sarafina, the lioness was already questioning her cub.

"What was the reason behind this, Nala?" Sarafina asked. "Did you think I would let you go frolicking around the savanna simply because Sarabi told me to?"

"No… I… I just…" Nala's voice broke.

"She wants to be like the other cubs," Sarabi answered for her.

Sarafina twisted around. "She is not like the other cubs. She is *my* cub. And I will do whatever I can to keep her safe. I will not end up like you."

Sarabi's head jerked back as gasps rang out from the other lionesses who stood around the clearing. It felt as if she had been slapped with sharp claws. Though Sarafina's claw would not have hurt her nearly as badly as her words had. She never could have imagined her best friend saying such an awful thing to her, but at least now she knew how Sarafina truly felt.

Sarabi lifted her chin in the air.

"I believe I will turn in for the night."

Fayola rushed to her side, but Sarabi held her off.

"No. I am okay," Sarabi said. "Continue celebrating with your cubs."

Projecting the strength she had been forced to display even on her darkest days, she turned and staunchly made her way back to Pride Rock.

CHAPTER SIX

Nala stood at the water's edge, quietly lapping at the communal water hole her pride shared with a number of other animals that resided in this area of the savanna. A family of giraffes drank just to her right, while a pack of okapis stood on the opposite bank across from her. There was an unspoken peace alliance between those who used this water source; Nala had never once witnessed a lioness attack another animal while here.

The water hole had become a place of refuge these past months, its peacefulness providing much-needed comfort. She usually enjoyed the feel of the moist earth beneath her paws, but she feared nothing would be able to lift her spirits today. A heavy cloud had fallen over Pride Rock after her mother and Sarabi's argument last night. There were subdued murmurs amongst the lionesses but none of the typical light-hearted chatter she was accustomed to when visiting the water hole.

Guilt sat in the pit of Nala's stomach like spoiled gazelle meat.

She was the reason for the shroud of unease that blanketed their home. If she had not asked Sarabi to intervene on her behalf, her mother would have never lashed out at her.

Nala still could not believe her mother had spoken to their queen in such a way. Sarabi was more than just her queen – she was her mother's best friend. And the hurtful words she had said... Nala wished she could go back in time so that she could prevent her mother from ever saying such ugly things.

But if she could go back in time, she would go back six months to when all their troubles began. She would stop Simba and Mufasa from travelling to the gorge. She would stop the wildebeests from launching their deadly stampede. She would change it all.

As she drank more water, Nala felt the fur on the back of her neck rise with a sense of alarm. She whipped around to find Ola and Kahina standing a few feet behind her. They stared at her with matching looks of disgust.

"What do you want?" Nala asked.

"First you ruin the Hunting Games, and now you have ruined the entire pride," Ola said. "We all know that Sarabi and Sarafina aren't talking because of you."

"It's not my fault," Nala said, even though that was untrue. All of this *was* her fault.

"My mother said Sarabi has not been this sad since she lost Simba," Kahina said.

Nala winced. The words cut deep because she knew how devastating losing Simba had been for all of them, especially his mother.

"I just wanted her to talk to my mother. I thought she could help," Nala whispered.

"Well, they talked," Ola said. "A lot of good that did."

"Leave her alone."

They all looked over to where the voice had come from. It was Puleng. The younger cub walked over to stand at Nala's side.

"You taunted her because she does not know how to hunt, and now you taunt her for trying to change things so she can learn to hunt? Nala thought Sarabi could make her mother see reason."

"Why are you defending her?" Ola asked.

"Yeah, she's older than you. Older cubs are supposed

to stick up for younger cubs, not the other way around," Kahina said.

That is what they had all been taught from a young age. As each new cub was born into their pride, it was the job of the older cubs to protect the younglings. Nala appreciated Puleng's willingness to stand up for her, but it would only bring more ridicule on her head.

"I don't need you to defend me," she told her.

Confused hurt flashed in the younger cub's eyes.

Just then, a lioness-shaped shadow fell over them. Nala looked up into her mother's piercing green eyes.

"Come with me, Nala. It is time for your bath," her mother said. She glanced at the other cubs. "Ola, Kahina, Puleng, go to your mothers. They are ready to bathe you as well."

Nala walked closely behind Sarafina, following her to the patch of lemongrass on the opposite side of the water hole where the other lionesses lounged in a loose circle. Her throat tightened when her mother settled well away from where Sarabi sat with her sister, Kito.

Nala's chest tightened with despair. The three lionesses always sat together while at the water hole. But now, because of her, her mother had isolated herself from them.

"Mum," Nala started, but then she stopped.

What could she say? That she was sorry?

Nala realised that, despite the fallout from last night's argument, she was *not* sorry she had asked Sarabi to intervene on her behalf. She had been desperate, and now she was even *more* desperate to find a solution to what had become an even more dire situation.

"It is time for your bath," Sarafina repeated, then began licking Nala's fur.

Nala noticed the other cubs going off to play once they were done with their baths, but she didn't bother to ask. Even if her mother gave her permission to join them, she would only be subjecting herself to more ridicule. Maybe she and Kamari could play once he returned to Pride Rock. His mother had taken him out for a pouncing lesson.

Just as Nala closed her eyes for a nap, she heard the rumbling of increasingly loud whispers travelling amongst the gathered lionesses.

News. A sighting. Rafiki sent word.

Nala felt her mother stiffen at the mention of the beloved mandrill who had served as the pride's healer for years. Rafiki had departed Pride Rock shortly after they'd lost Simba and Mufasa, and he had not been heard from since.

Nala strained to hear what was being said, but the lionesses were doing that thing they did when they thought whatever was being discussed was too much for the cubs to deal with. Speaking in hushed tones, several of them glanced her way. Their furtive, concerned looks confirmed what Nala had already suspected.

It was news. Big news. Important news.

When she saw the dwarf mongoose who was known to be one of the scouting animals Sarabi had dispatched to gather information from around the savanna and beyond, any doubts were erased. He stood on a boulder so that he could look their queen directly in the eye as he imparted whatever news he'd brought back. By the look of things, it was serious.

"What could it be?" Fayola asked loud enough for Nala to hear.

"Do you really think there has been a sighting?" Sefu added.

Once again Nala felt her mother stiffen.

"It has been quite some time since we have heard anything," Fayola murmured. "At least four weeks."

"Longer," Sefu said. "The last time we got word of Simba being seen, it was just after the swallows began their migration north."

Thandi, who had been close enough to Sarabi to hear what the mongoose was saying, approached them.

"Thandi, what is going on?" Sefu asked.

"There is news of another sighting," she confirmed. "Of course, it is difficult to say if it is Simba, but the mongoose also reports that Rafiki had a vision."

All the lionesses, including Nala's mother, stood at this. Rafiki's visions were not to be disputed. They always confirmed or revealed something.

"What did he see?" Sarafina asked.

As far as Nala knew, this was the first time her mother had spoken to any of the lionesses since last night. Sefu, Thandi and Fayola all stared at her for several moments before Thandi spoke.

"He had a vision of Simba with two others... in a cave," she said. "One figure was stout and the other was slim, but Rafiki could not make out who or what they were."

A smattering of murmurs rattled amongst them as the lionesses dissected this bit of information. Her mother had gone back to being silent, her ears erect as she appeared to be listening intently to the shared theories of what Rafiki must have seen.

All of a sudden there was a commotion coming from Sarabi's direction. Several of the lionesses ran over there, but Nala's mother stayed back. Nala climbed up on a rock to see if she could discern what was happening.

Sarabi was shaking her head while Kito and Sefu tried to talk to her.

"I don't want to hear about any more of these sightings!" Sarabi screamed.

Nala flinched at the raw emotion in her voice. Their queen was always so calm, so stoic. It was rare to hear her raise her voice at all and even rarer to hear such pain in it.

"I cannot take any more of this," Sarabi said. "These sightings never lead to anything. Only more fissures in my heart."

Nala heard a strangled cry coming from her mother. She looked over and saw the distress on her face. She could tell she wanted to go comfort Sarabi.

Go! Nala wanted to say, but she couldn't say anything. *She* was the reason her mother didn't feel comfortable being near her very best friend right now.

After several tension-filled moments had passed, their queen stood up straight and lifted her face in that dignified, regal way of hers. She returned to where the dwarf mongoose still stood atop the boulder.

"Thank you for the information you have shared," Sarabi told him. "I will not require you to bring back any more information about Simba from this day forward. It is time I accept that my son is gone."

"Sarabi, you don't know that," Kito said.

"He is gone," she stated in a voice that brooked no argument.

A hush fell over the lionesses who had gathered around. When Scar had come back from the gorge with the horrible news of Mufasa's and Simba's deaths, the despair had been instant and intense. But when members of the pride had gone to retrieve their bodies and had only come upon Mufasa's, the hope that Simba had miraculously survived the stampede clung to their pride the way catchweed clung to fur. Even as the days dragged on into weeks and into months, no one wanted to give up on that hope.

But now Sarabi had done just that.

With their queen's pronouncement, they would all have to accept that the search for Simba was over. There was no longer any hope that he had survived, no hope that he was ever coming back to Pride Rock.

Nala's heart felt as if it would break apart into thousands of pieces.

She caught sight of Sarabi making her way towards them, her steps slow and deliberate, her eyes straight ahead. Nala glanced over at her mother and saw the way she tracked her best friend's movements, her eyes following her as she walked back to Pride Rock. Her sadness was too deep to disguise.

Sarafina rose and started to follow Sarabi, but two of the other lionesses stopped her.

"Not now, Sarafina," Kito said.

"I just… I want to—"

"Not now," the lionesses repeated. "She wants to be

alone. Let her have her space."

Nala could sense how badly her mother wanted to offer comfort to Sarabi and how much it hurt her that she couldn't. Nala was unsure if Sarabi would even accept any gesture her mother made towards her, and that saddened her more than anything. The two were usually inseparable, but Nala had found a way to separate them.

"Why did she call off the search?" Fayola asked Kito. "There's always a chance that Simba will be found."

"Do you really think that?" Kito asked. "Do any of us really think that? We have all been holding on to hope because it is what Sarabi needed, but if we are being honest, we know how improbable it is that Simba has been able to survive out there on his own for such a long time. He was but a cub when he was taken from us. It is over."

"I agree," Thandi said. "Especially after learning where he was supposedly spotted this time. There is no way Simba made it all the way there."

"Where?" Sefu asked.

And then Nala heard the one word that changed everything.

Garamba.

CHAPTER SEVEN

The mood around Pride Rock was even more sombre than it had been earlier in the day, before the dwarf mongoose had come bearing news about Rafiki's vision and another Simba sighting. There were whispers amongst the other cubs, who had all been away during Sarabi's outburst. For once, Nala's opinion was in demand amongst them as she was the only cub who had witnessed it all first-paw.

"So she just won't look for Simba anymore?" Puleng asked.

Nala shook her head. "She told the mongoose that she doesn't want to receive any further reports."

The other cubs remained quiet – even Ola, whom Nala had been expecting to make some kind of nasty remark.

"Does this mean that Scar will be the king of Pride Rock forever?" Bontu asked.

"No, eventually Kamari will take his place as king," Kahina said. "At least I *think* that is what will happen, since Kamari is Kito's son and Kito is Sarabi's sister."

They continued with their discussion about the line of succession, but Nala didn't participate. For one, she hated when there was talk of anyone other than Simba leading their pride. More important, Nala wasn't ready to give up hope just yet. Not after hearing the location of this latest sighting.

Ever since they'd first heard zebras at the water hole recounting all the glorious things they had seen on their migration, Nala and Simba had talked about leaving Pride Rock and going on a grand adventure. They wanted to experience the rushing waterfalls of Rusumo and run across the sand dunes in Napeget.

But of all the places they dreamt of going, Garamba was the one they talked about the most. Its lush tropical forests, rushing rivers and massive grasslands sounded like the best playground a cub could ever want to live in.

It was the reason Nala had always dismissed news of other sightings that had been brought back to them these last six months. Because she knew that if Simba had somehow survived the violent wildebeest stampede that day in the gorge, and for some reason had not returned to Pride Rock, the only other place he would have travelled was Garamba.

Hearing that the mongoose had mentioned Garamba, the place she and Simba had promised to visit, had more than piqued her interest. Together with the other titbit that had been reported just a few minutes prior – that Rafiki had 'seen' Simba not merely in the jungle but in a cave – it was all but confirmed for her.

It had to be the Blue Grotto.

Once they'd heard about Garamba, she and Simba had set out to learn everything they could about the forest. The one place all the animals talked about most enthusiastically was the Blue Grotto. By all accounts, it was one of the most beautiful places in all Africa.

It had to be more than just a coincidence that Rafiki's vision and this latest sighting both pointed to the same place.

Could Simba really be there?

Nervous excitement made the fur on the back of Nala's neck stand on end. Just the thought of what it would mean if Simba was truly alive was enough to make her want to run around in a circle and shout for joy.

Instead, Nala kept her expression as sombre as the others'. She could not share her thoughts with any of the other cubs – not yet. No one knew of her and Simba's secret dreams of visiting Garamba. They would accuse her of trying to get Sarabi's hopes up when their queen had already stated that she no longer wanted to pursue clues about Simba.

It was the last thing Nala wanted to do. Sarabi had suffered enough.

Later that night, Nala lay in the crook of her mother's foreleg. Several of the other lionesses had once again gone on a hunt, and this time Kahina and Ola had been allowed to go with them as part of their reward for winning the Hunting Games. They had now graduated to another level in their training.

Nala had been upset, but only for a moment. She had more important things to think about than hunting. Like what, if anything, she should do about this latest Simba sighting.

That was the first question. Should she do anything about it? Should she say anything at all?

She had considered going to Sefu or Kito, but she was just too unsure of what their reaction would be. Now that Sarabi had made her desires known, Nala was almost certain that the lionesses would shut down any talk about further pursuing what the dwarf mongoose had brought back to them. There had been too many false leads already, and just because she and Simba had talked about visiting Garamba one day, it wouldn't be enough of a reason for the lionesses to believe it would lead to anything at this time.

Maybe *she* shouldn't believe it either.

This was probably just like all the other sightings – some lion cub who was Simba's age and who had been separated or banished from his own pride. That's what all the other reports of news had turned out to be.

She was already looked upon with scorn by many in her pride; how much worse would it be if she were to give them false hope, only for it to turn out that Simba wasn't in Garamba after all…

But what if she went to find him on her own?

A jolt of eager excitement shot through her, shaking her entire body.

"Nala, go to sleep," her mother admonished in a drowsy voice.

Nala settled back into the crook of her mother's leg, but she could not settle her suddenly racing thoughts.

What if she went in search of Simba and was able to bring their pride's true king back to Pride Rock? She would be seen as a hero instead of Sarafina's sheltered little baby cub.

But this was so much bigger than just her. This would impact their entire pride. How different would life around here be if Simba ruled Pride Rock instead of Scar?

The first thing he would do would be to run the hyenas off. The Pride Lands would go back to being the verdant home they had all enjoyed before everything changed. Her mother and Sarabi would go back to being the friends they had once been as they would have no cause to fight anymore, because Sarafina would have no reason to be so protective of Nala, not with their rightful king's safe return. If Nala could somehow travel to Garamba and find Simba alive, it could change everything.

Nala shook her head.

It was foolish for her to even think such thoughts. She wasn't allowed to travel past the water hole; how could she possibly think that she could make it all the way to Garamba? She didn't know the first thing about how to get there.

Except… she did.

During many of their jaunts around the Pride Lands, she and Simba had mapped out the path to Garamba. Based on information they had gathered from animals who had been there, they had determined that they were to follow the grouping of stars that looked like the mighty Abigar cattle that grazed around the savanna. As long as those stars remained straight ahead, they would take them directly to that lush jungle they had dreamt of visiting.

But that didn't mean she could get there on her own. Even if she managed to sneak away without her mother's realising it, and then make it to Garamba, how would she find Simba there? By all accounts, Garamba was massive. It would be difficult for a fully grown lioness to get there and survive on her own; a lion cub who didn't know how to hunt would face certain death.

Nala settled more securely against her mother and stared at the walls of the cave where they slept.

She was safe here at Pride Rock. And if Simba was actually spotted in Garamba, there was no guarantee that he would still be there if she were to go in search of him. She could spend her life combing the entire savanna and never find him.

Yes, it was best she stay right here where she was safe. They had all adjusted to this new life on Pride Rock so far, and they would continue to do so.

CHAPTER EIGHT

"Quick, gather the cubs!"

The panic-stricken voice startled Nala out of an already fitful night's sleep, driving her heart to beat fast against her chest. She tried to stand, but her wobbly legs wouldn't cooperate. The sudden chaos surrounding her made it even more difficult to find her bearings as lionesses dashed frenziedly around the cavernous space.

"Sarafina, bring the cubs deeper into the cave. Keep them hidden!" Sefu ordered.

"What's going on?" Nala asked.

Her mother didn't answer but clamped her mouth on the back of Nala's neck and hauled her into the innermost part of the cave. Nala watched with a growing sense of dread as Sarafina then did the same with the rest of the cubs.

"What's going on?" she asked Kamari, who had just been deposited next to her.

"It's the hyenas," he whispered. "They're on the attack."

The hyenas. She should have known.

Their pride had no natural predators in this kingdom – other than the lion prides that prowled in search of new shelters – but none of them would be so bold as to attack Pride Rock. Only the hyenas would do such a thing, and they were now part of the kingdom.

When Scar took over as king and pronounced that their kingdom would be merged with that of those awful hyenas, the entire pride had protested. How could mortal enemies be expected to coexist? They hunted the same prey, and worse, the hyenas often targeted lion cubs when in search of food. Those flea-infested dogs were the pride's fiercest competition in nearly every aspect of their lives.

But Scar would not listen to the lionesses' concerns. He had welcomed the hyenas into the kingdom and had banished the two remaining lions who had been part of their pride following the deaths of Mufasa and Simba, leaving Kamari as the only male. No one talked about it, but Nala knew they all feared that Scar would send him away once he came of age.

What Scar had promised would be a great and glorious

future between the lions and hyenas had proved to be as horrific as the lionesses had predicted. Pride Rock's new, unwelcome residents had brought nothing but destruction to their home.

Nala could hear the racket of riotous peals and howls even from deep within the cave. Sefu, Sarabi, Kito, Fayola and Thandi rushed over to where they all were huddled.

"Are the cubs all safe?" Thandi asked Sarafina.

"Yes. Is it the hyenas?" Nala's mother asked.

Sefu nodded. "They are raiding last night's kill. They are going to take it all if we don't put a stop to it."

Nala ran over to her mother and buried her face against her fur. She twisted around far enough to watch through the corner of her eye as Sarabi assumed her place in the centre of the lionesses.

"The hyenas are on the attack." She looked around at the lionesses. "We all know what this means, and that there is a possibility all will not return. Sarafina and Fayola will remain with the cubs. The rest of us will defend the kill."

"You should stay here with the others," Kito said to Sarabi.

"No," Sarabi said. "I will defend the kill."

"Sarabi—"

"I will not argue with you," the queen said.

The lionesses all fell in line behind her; then, as a group, they sprinted out of the cave. Sarafina pulled Puleng and Kamari in close, protecting them while their mothers went out to protect the pride.

Nala once again buried her face against her mother's chest. She could hear the hideous sound of ripping flesh as the lionesses battled with the hyenas. There was a loud, awful cry that Nala was certain came from one of the lionesses. Moments later, Sefu returned to the cave, dragging a limping Thandi behind her.

"Tend to her leg," Sefu said before darting back out.

Sarafina went to her side, but Thandi held her off. "I am okay. Stay with the cubs."

"How many hyenas are there?" Fayola asked.

"Two dozen, at least."

"This cannot continue," the other lioness said. "Why does he allow them to stay?"

There was another scream. This one sounded like Sarabi.

Sarafina shot up. "Take care of the cubs. I'm going to help."

"Mama, no!" Nala screamed and ran to her, grabbing on to her leg.

"Stay where you are," Thandi said to Sarafina. "Sarabi gave you your orders."

"My pride needs me!"

"To protect our cubs so that our pride lives on!" Thandi shouted. "Do as your queen ordered!"

Suddenly a loud roar echoed against the walls of the cave, putting a halt to Sarafina and Thandi's dispute and bringing the outside fighting to an abrupt end. Nala could hear the scramble of feet racing away, no doubt the hyenas retreating to the holes they'd crawled out of. They were as cowardly as they were destructive.

"Where are the others?" came Scar's angry voice. "Come out of that cave at once!"

Nala's legs trembled. She looked to the other cubs and saw they were just as frightened as she was.

"Come," her mother said to her. "All of you."

"But—" Nala started.

"Come," Sarafina repeated. "Scar will not harm you. I will not let him."

And Nala knew in that moment that her mother would fight Scar to the death before she allowed him to harm her or any of the other cubs. All the lionesses would do so, even those who did not have cubs of their own.

They filed out of the cave. Nala had to blink several times to adjust her eyes to the brightening sun. She hated to admit the fear she felt as she watched Scar pace slowly in front of the lionesses lined up against the wall of stone.

His tail swished back and forth behind him, its lazy cadence a stark contrast to the furor in his eyes.

"Now," Scar said. "What is the meaning of all this fighting? Didn't I proclaim that there would be peace here on Pride Rock?"

Sarabi took several steps forwards, a clear indication of her role as their queen. When she spoke, it was with an air of authority.

"The lionesses spent much of the night replenishing the food stores, and those hyenas came in this morning and tried to steal it all."

"Sarabi, Sarabi, Sarabi," Scar sang in a deceptively sweet voice. "How can the hyenas steal something that also belongs to them? We are all family, remember?"

"They are not our family," Sarabi said. "And we cannot continue to exert this much effort to find food, only to have the hyenas consume the entire kill. The lionesses are exhausted. They are having to go further and further out to hunt."

"The Pride Lands are filled with prey. They are simply searching in the wrong places. I would not be surprised if they are doing so purposely."

"The lionesses are doing all they can to secure food. There is none," Sarabi said. "The dry season has lasted much longer than it has in years past. Do you not see what this drought has done to the grasslands? There is hardly anything left for the animals to graze on. Many have left in search of water. Couple that with the hyenas' ferocious appetites and the lionesses cannot keep up."

"What about the cubs?" Scar asked. "Make them hunt."

"They are not ready."

"Well, make them ready!" he bellowed. "I want every cub in this pride to go out and hunt, starting tonight."

Sarafina gasped and wrapped a paw around Nala.

"You are putting them in danger," Sarabi said. She shut her eyes for several moments, then said, "It is possible that three of the cubs are ready to take on a more active role in hunting, but I refuse to send out the younger cubs. I will not allow it."

Nala's breath caught in her throat as Scar closed the distance between himself and Sarabi. She heard low growls coming from several of the lionesses.

"*You* will not allow it?" Scar asked. "You are forgetting who rules this kingdom, Sarabi. *I* do. Now, go out there and hunt. You lionesses had no problem hunting for food when Mufasa was here."

"We hunted the same amount," Thandi said. "The difference is that Mufasa would never have allowed hyenas to live at Pride Rock."

Scar raced over to her, his face inches from hers.

"Hunt more," he said with a low growl. "Because the hyenas are here to stay."

He took several steps back and tried to take on an apologetic tone.

"My dear lionesses, why are we fighting? I thought we had come to an understanding. I have explained that the hyenas are our friends. It is time the rest of you accepted it."

"Friends do not raid the food of their friends, or threaten their young," Sarabi pointed out.

"It was one time," Scar said. "No cubs were hurt." He released a dramatic sigh and rolled his eyes. "Look, we all want what is best for Pride Rock. We have to learn to live together. It should not be this difficult."

"The food sources will be depleted if the hyenas remain, Scar," Sarabi said. "That is a fact. This is not sustainable."

"Make it sustainable," he said, all traces of his previous contriteness gone. "You have no other choice." He ambled slowly along the line of lionesses, looking each in the eye, including the cubs. "Now," Scar said once he'd reached the end of the line, "why don't we all get some rest? You lionesses have a long night of hunting ahead of you."

The tension in the air was thick as they all stood silently and watched Scar saunter back towards his cave on the other end of Pride Rock. The lionesses took a collective breath once he was gone.

Thandi limped over to Sarabi and nudged her with her nose. "Are you okay?"

"Are any of us okay?" was Sarabi's reply. "The hyenas are making Pride Rock uninhabitable. How much longer will we be able to survive here?"

No one refuted her statement because they all knew it was the truth. It had become more apparent with each day that passed.

"Mufasa would be so disappointed in me if he knew what I had allowed our home to become," Sarabi continued.

"No, he would not," Thandi argued.

"He would never," Sefu added, running up to her side. "Mufasa was always proud of you. You are doing your best."

"You cannot blame yourself for the pain Scar has caused," Kito said. "This is his doing, not yours."

Several of the other lionesses joined them, all assuring Sarabi that she was not at fault for what had become of Pride Rock. Nala looked to her mother, who stared at her fellow pridemates with a forlorn expression. But she did not join them. Instead, she circled back around the cubs, bringing them all together against her.

"What are we going to do about last night's kill?" Thandi asked. "The hyenas made away with most of it."

"We have more pressing matters to contend with," Sarabi said. She closed her eyes and sucked in a deep breath. When she opened them again, she took the time to look at all the lionesses surrounding her. "There is something that we have all been avoiding, but it cannot go unsaid any longer. We will have to leave Pride Rock."

A collective gasp sounded throughout the group.

"No," Nala whispered.

"We cannot leave," Sefu argued.

"We cannot stay. Not for much longer," Sarabi said. "I do not want to leave either, but we cannot go on this way. Look at how long it took to secure last night's kill. And within seconds, those hyenas made away with it. We cannot live this way much longer."

"But this is our home," Kito said. "We cannot relinquish it to the hyenas."

"We will have no choice. Unless Scar steps up and becomes the type of king we need him to be, we will have to go in search of another home."

Unease wove its way through the pack of lionesses as the reality of their dire situation began to settle in. It felt as if a raging windstorm had blown through, devastating the entire pride.

Fear sank into Nala's heart like a mighty claw sinking into its prey. She had considered life beyond Pride Rock a number of times in the past, but with the knowledge that she would always be able to return. Never once had she thought they would be forced to leave. It was unthinkable. This was *their* home. It was their source of protection and comfort. They could not allow those awful hyenas to run them away.

There was only one way to stop that from happening: she must find Simba and bring him back to Pride Rock. Simba was the rightful king; it was his by birthright. And he was the only one who could rightfully remove Scar from the throne.

If Simba was dead, Scar's rule would have to continue. But if there was any truth to Rafiki's vision – if Simba was out there somewhere – then he would be able to save them all.

She just had to find him first.

CHAPTER NINE

Nala lay with her chin on her paws, feigning sleep as Kito stood watch at the opening of the cave that served as the lionesses' sleeping quarters. The *drip, drip, drip* of droplets from a thunderstorm that had taken them all by surprise produced an eerie song as they fell onto Pride Rock's slick stone.

It had been a long, sombre day, one of the darkest since the day they lost Mufasa and Simba – and not only because of the rain shower. Sarabi's pronouncement had shrouded the entire pride in sadness, and the looming threat of the hyenas had them all on edge.

Nala's mother had been even more overprotective than usual following the early morning raid. She demanded Nala remain at her side as she tended to the injuries of several of the lionesses who had been hurt while fighting the hyenas. If Nala moved just a few feet away, her mother was tugging her back to her side.

More than half of the lionesses had gone out to hunt tonight, along with all the cubs except for Nala, Puleng and Abena. Despite the large number of hunters, they had only managed to capture a couple of hares and a small kudu. It wasn't enough to feed on for a day.

Sarabi had been right in her assessment. Their resources were becoming more and more scarce, and the lionesses were having to travel much too far in order to secure food. They could not continue this way.

Nala tilted her head to the side as though trying to find a more comfortable sleeping position. She squinted at her mother through narrowed eyes. Taking care of her injured pridemates must have tired her out even more than Nala had first suspected. She slept so soundly that she had not noticed when Nala had gingerly wiggled out from underneath her paw.

Nala's next feat would be to wiggle her way out of this cave.

She had made the decision to leave just after the cubs had been brought in for the night. Given the circumstances her pride now found itself in, it was the only choice she could make. If there was any chance at all that Simba was still alive, she had to do whatever she could to find him and bring him back to Pride Rock.

She had taken note of the cloudless sky while they were still in the clearing earlier that evening. The thunder-storm had pushed out just as quickly as it had rushed in, leaving the ground nourished and the sky crystal clear.

Nala saw it as a sign that she was doing the right thing. The bull-shaped cluster of stars shone brightly, ready to guide her towards Garamba.

If she managed to slip past Thandi and Kito.

Sarabi had ordered the two lionesses to keep watch over the food that had been captured during tonight's hunt. Though instead of concentrating solely on the cave where the food was stored, Thandi and Kito took turns roaming between the smaller cave and the larger one where the lionesses slept with their cubs. Nala understood why they were hesitant to leave the sleeping quarters unguarded, but it only made things trickier for her.

But Nala had noticed a pattern. Thandi always took a bit longer to return to her post at the mouth of the cave. If Nala made her move the moment Kito went to fetch Thandi from the other cave, she could sneak out without either of the lionesses seeing her.

She tracked Kito's steps as Kito marched from one end

of the opening of the cave to the other. Nala's heart pounded like zebra hooves slapping against the dirt, but she made sure to keep her body as still as possible, impatiently waiting for her opportunity to flee. Although no lionesses were officially tasked with watching over the pride tonight, all the lionesses were likely on alert after the earlier encounter with the hyenas. If she made even the tiniest wrong move, she would probably awaken the entire pride. Her plan would be quashed before she had the chance to make it off Pride Rock.

Nala heard whispers at the front of the cave. She lifted one eyelid so she could get a better look at what was happening. Kito and Thandi stood with their heads close together, their attention on something to the right of Pride Rock.

One of the cubs whimpered in their sleep, and Kito twisted around to stare into the cave. She seemed to look directly at Nala.

No. No. No.

Nala shut her eyes tight and listened, waiting for the moment when Kito would jostle Sarafina awake to inquire why Nala was not sleeping.

But the other lioness never came for her.

She opened her eyes to find both Kito and Thandi gone from the mouth of the cave.

This was it.

This was her best chance to leave Pride Rock without any of the lionesses or cubs noticing. They would all realise she was missing in the morning, of course, but she would be well on her way to Garamba by then. If she was going to do this, she had to do it right now.

Nala looked over at her mother's sleeping form once again and had to hold in the sob that nearly escaped. Her mother would be upset, but even more than that, she would be terrified at the thought of Nala gone. As much as she disagreed with the way her mother had been treating her lately, Nala didn't want to cause her more worry. She could picture her going on a frantic search the moment she discovered Nala was missing.

That was why she would have to move as quickly as possible. She would also have to make sure she didn't leave a trail that could be easily followed.

Closing her eyes, Nala pulled in another deep breath. She needed to calm the nerves fluttering around in her belly. If she didn't, her legs would wobble too much for her to make it off Pride Rock.

She slid further away from her mother, staying on her stomach and moving as quietly as possible. Kahina mewled as Nala slid past her. She stopped, making sure the other cub was still sleeping before continuing towards the mouth of the cave.

Nala's eyes darted back and forth between the sleeping lionesses and cubs and the opening of the cave. She had no idea where Thandi and Kito had run off to, but she had no doubt they would be back soon. They had been ordered by Sarabi to keep watch, and no matter what had grabbed their attention, neither would deliberately defy their queen by staying away from their post for too long.

She inched along the floor like a stealth cheetah, not making a sound. Once she reached the opening of the cave, Nala peeked out.

It was clear.

She took a second to glance back at her mother, but she knew she did not have time to dwell on what would happen when they all realised Nala was gone. They would forgive her once she returned to Pride Rock with their rightful king.

Heartened by the image of Sarabi reuniting with Simba and what Simba's return would mean to their pride's existence – they would be able to remain in their home! – Nala took off. She travelled in the opposite direction from where Thandi and Kito had been looking, squeezing past boulders that had shifted because of the drought as she made her way down the side of Pride Rock.

Nala could hardly believe it when she reached the base of the rock formation. She looked up at the imposing facade; it took her breath away.

She'd done it. She had actually done it! She'd managed to slip away.

Now all she had to do was make it to the grasslands, where it would be harder for anyone to spot her if they were to wake up and look out over the Pride Lands. She glanced back at Pride Rock several times as she traversed the muddy clearing, keeping her head low.

She hoped she didn't encounter any animals at the water hole. She'd considered travelling a different route, but it would take too much time. She also was certain Thandi and Kito had gone off in the opposite direction. The last thing she wanted to do was run into either of them.

Nala kept her eye out for movement as she approached the water hole, but there wasn't a single animal around. She took it as yet another sign that she was doing the right thing; even the obstacles she had anticipated had been cleared from her path.

She hastened her steps, moving swiftly past the water hole. The tension in her shoulders began to ease as she caught sight of the taller grasses straight ahead. Yet the closer she got to the grasslands, the more her apprehension grew.

She was really doing this. She was leaving the only home she knew, leaving the safety of her pride and venturing out into the vastness of Africa.

All on her own.

What are you doing?

What if those stories she and Simba had heard about the stars were wrong and they *didn't* lead to Garamba? What if Rafiki's vision had been cloudy? What if she made it off the Pride Lands and got lost going through that creepy Elephant Graveyard? There were so many things that could go wrong.

But what if things went right?

Nala sat up on her hind legs and stared straight ahead at the tall grass.

She was the only one who knew of Simba's plans to visit Garamba. It was up to her to find him and bring him home. It was up to her to save her pride.

"You're doing this," she said in a fierce whisper. For the last six months, her mother's fears had wreaked havoc in her life, but Nala refused to allow fear to hold her back. Determined to see this through, she charged forwards.

"Nala?"

Nala froze.

No way had she been seen. She had been too careful.

"Nala! Wait for me!"

She turned and nearly screamed at the sight of Abena scampering across the clearing towards her.

"Abena, what are you doing here?" Nala asked as the younger cub approached.

"You couldn't sleep either, huh?" Abena asked. "Neither could I. Every time I close my eyes, I see the hyenas coming after me with their bloody fangs and drool dripping from their mouths." She shivered. "And their eyes are yellow like cassia flowers. They're scary. Don't you think they're scary?"

"How did you find me?"

"I told you I couldn't sleep. I saw when you left the cave. Then I saw your footsteps in the mud, so I just followed them."

So much for being a stealthy cheetah.

She also hadn't anticipated her footsteps leaving a muddy trail that would point the lionesses in her direction in the morning. For a moment, Nala considered going back and creating some kind of divergence, but she didn't have time. It was better to keep moving forwards. The sooner she could put more distance between herself and Pride Rock, the harder it would be for them to catch up with her.

"I want to go for a walk with you," Abena said.

"I'm not—" Nala stopped herself before she spilled all her plans. "I want to walk alone. I don't want any company."

"Please, Nala. I'm too afraid to walk by myself."

Just then, Nala heard what sounded like a shout coming from Pride Rock.

"Get down," she said to Abena, crouching low to the ground. A moment later, a bird flew overheard, cawing as it swooped around their heads.

"It's just a bird," Nala said with a sigh of relief.

"Ola's right. You really *are* afraid of everything," Abena said.

Nala growled at her. It was bad enough she had to take this stuff from the older cubs. She wasn't going to put up with it from the runt of their pride.

"Go back to the cave," Nala ordered her.

"Not until after our walk," Abena said. "I won't sleep anyway, so it's just as well if I join you."

"No!" Ugh! Why was she so stubborn?

Nala looked back at Pride Rock to make sure no one had heard her before turning her attention back to Abena. In her most forceful voice, she said, "You can't come with me, so just go back."

The cub tilted her head to the side and narrowed her eyes. "You weren't going on a walk, were you? Where are you going?"

Nala gritted her teeth at Abena's reaction to her forceful voice. It was entirely wrong: Where was the cowering and shivering in fear? Though to say that she was the youngest of the pride overlooked that the cub was way too smart.

"Come on, Nala. Tell me!"

What was she supposed to do now? If she sent Abena back, the cub would probably wake up the other lionesses. Or, even worse, what if Thandi and Kito had returned to their posts? They would question why Abena was out and about and would learn that Nala was gone too.

She had no choice but to tell her something.

But she could not reveal she was going in search of Simba or that she suspected she knew where he might be. No one could know any of that. Nala didn't want to get any of the lionesses' hopes up, just in case the latest sighting turned out to be like all the others. And even if Simba was in Garamba, she wasn't sure she was heading in the right direction. *Please let the stars lead me the right way.*

"I'm going on an adventure," Nala told Abena. "Alone."

"An adventure!" Abena squealed.

"Shhhh," Nala hissed. "Keep it down."

"I've always wanted to go on an adventure. Can we see Lake Victoria? I heard it is bigger than all the Pride Lands."

"No lake is as big as the Pride Lands," Nala said. "And no, I'm not going to Lake Victoria. And no, you cannot follow me. I told you I am going on this adventure alone. Go back to Pride Rock, and do not tell anyone you saw me, Abena. I mean it."

Nala turned and continued towards the grasslands. She'd taken only a couple of steps when a soft plea stopped her.

"Please."

Nala spun around to find Abena standing in the spot

where she had left her, head hung low.

"Please," the younger cub repeated. "Let me come on the adventure with you. I never get to do anything."

Nala wanted to point out that Abena had been allowed to do even more than she had. Yet, because she had been held back at Pride Rock while the other cubs went off for pouncing lessons or playing in the scrubland past the water hole, Nala understood how the young cub felt.

She looked out towards the wide expanse that stretched before her and acknowledged that the thought of travelling across it alone made her stomach queasy. Would it be so bad to have a companion?

"Okay, you can join me on my adventure," Nala said. "But there are rules you have to follow."

Abena's head bobbed with enthusiasm.

"You have to do what I say," Nala told her.

She frowned. "If you're gonna boss me around like all the others, then I'm not going." She turned and started stomping back towards Pride Rock.

Nala reached out with her paw and clamped down on her tail, pinning it to the ground.

"Stop," she said. She jogged around to face the younger cub. "It's not bossing you around; I'm not the queen like Sarabi. I just want to make sure we're both safe."

"What if *I* see something dangerous?"

"Then I'll listen to you," Nala said.

Abena's eyes widened. "You will?"

Nala nodded. "It will be a partnership. But no running ahead of me. We must stick together."

"What about fireflies?"

Nala frowned. "What about them?"

"If we see a cloud of fireflies, we have to stop and play with them. That's my rule."

Some rule, Nala wanted to say. But she only nodded.

"Fine, we'll stop for fireflies," Nala said.

"Okay, let's go!" Abena said. She took off, running ahead of Nala although Nala had specifically told her not to do that very thing.

Nala looked up at the stars and let out a sigh.

She was going to regret this. She was sure of it.

CHAPTER TEN

The tall reeds bent forwards like giraffes bowing before their king as Nala and Abena hiked through the grasslands. Tonight's rain had not had the same effect on this area as it had on the clearing. The grass had acted as a barrier, preventing the rain from completely saturating the ground, so there was less mud, which meant fewer tracks.

Still, Nala continued to glance behind them every few steps to make sure the taller grass bounced back into place as they travelled through it. She had been both excited and relieved when she'd realised they would be able to slink through the grasslands without leaving a trail.

The moonlight beamed down, illuminating their path ahead but also casting shadows whenever they passed a tree. Nala did her best not to get too creeped out by it. The shadows made the trees seem even more ominous.

It's just a tree.

No wonder the other cubs thought she was afraid of everything. She was! When had she become such a scaredy-cat?

What happened to that brave cub who would go up against the future king of their pride with all the confidence in the world? Back when Simba was here, there was never a challenge she would not face, never a dare she would back down from. How had she allowed herself to become such a coward?

But she knew how it had happened. Her mother's fears had become her own without her even realising it. Nala had rolled her eyes every time her mother cautioned her against doing the simplest thing for fear that it was too dangerous, but somehow she had started to believe it all.

Well, she was done being a coward. A coward would not make it past the scrubland. If she was going to reach Garamba, she would have to look deep inside and find the fearless cub she used to be.

And she would have to find her quickly, because if her memory served her correctly, she and Abena were nearing the Elephant Graveyard.

Nala glanced up at the sky to confirm that the bull-shaped

cluster of stars was still directly in front of her. She was unsure what she would do once the sun came up. They could not spend the entire day sheltered, waiting for the stars to come out again, but she also did not want to get too far off track during daylight hours.

Maybe there was a river she could follow. Rivers moved in relatively straight lines, didn't they?

"This adventure is boring," Abena said. "I thought you were supposed to do fun things on an adventure. So far all we've done is walk."

"You asked to come along," Nala said. "You don't get to complain just because you're not having fun."

"But that doesn't make sense. When else would I complain? I wouldn't have to complain if I was having fun."

"You don't get to complain at all," Nala told her.

"That's not one of the rules," Abena complained.

"I'm making it a rule."

"Well, I'm making it a rule that we have to sing while we walk, because this is boring."

"No!" Nala said, lowering her voice to a whisper, even though they were well beyond where any of the lionesses on Pride Rock could hear them. They were so far away now that the peak of the rock formation they called home could barely be seen. Still, she wasn't taking any chances.

"No singing," she said to Abena. "Believe me, it

won't be boring for much longer."

Not that it would be much fun either.

Nala knew they were nearing the edge of the Pride Lands, which meant they were close to the end of the easy portion of their journey to Garamba. And the first difficult task lay just beyond the rise at the northern edge of the Pride Lands. She could still remember the cold, dark shadowy land. It made her shiver just thinking about it.

Please be alive, Simba. Don't let me go through this for nothing.

They reached the Elephant Graveyard not long after they cleared the scrubland.

"Whoa. What is this place?" Abena asked, her voice shaking as she stared out at the miles and miles of decaying skeletons.

"They call it the Shadowlands," Nala said. And it looked a thousand times creepier at night than it had the afternoon she and Simba had sneaked away to see it.

Smoke rose from the natural geysers that dotted the landscape. In the quiet of the late night, Nala could hear the steaming water percolating just below the earth's surface. Even those geysers were scary.

"It's an Elephant Graveyard," she explained to Abena. "This is where the hyenas lived before King Scar brought them to Pride Rock."

Abena took several steps back. "Are there any hyenas still living here?"

"I don't think so," Nala said. Although, to be honest, she didn't know what lived here. Maybe some of the hyenas had been left behind. Maybe something else had moved here in their place, like snakes. She hated snakes.

I'm not afraid of anything.

She heard Simba's voice in her head, so cocky and clear that Nala could have sworn he was standing right next to her. She hadn't been afraid of anything when Simba was around. Or if she was afraid of something, she would never let it show. She had been more afraid of her best friend thinking she was a coward than anything she would encounter down in that dusty basin.

"Why did you want to come *here* for an adventure?" Abena asked. "The lake would have been better."

"This isn't the adventure," Nala said. "Well, I guess it's part of it. But there's more to my adventure than the Elephant Graveyard."

Nala looked up at the stars.

Maybe she could figure out a way to go beyond these Shadowlands without going through them.

But she knew she couldn't. She didn't have time. Daylight would be upon them soon, and if she found herself off course without the guidance of the stars, it could cause her to lose even more time. They would have to go this way.

"You said you were bored. I'll bet you won't say that again," she told Abena. "Come on." They started down the sloping embankment. "Careful where you step," Nala called over her shoulder. "One wrong move and you can go sliding all the way down."

She knew that from experience.

The air grew warmer the closer they got to the floor of the basin. And just as she remembered, a blanketing mist hovered in the air above them. It was thin enough for Nala to make out the stars, but the way the moon's soft glow illuminated it made this graveyard even creepier.

"I'm scared," Abena said, putting voice to the feeling Nala hadn't wanted to acknowledge.

For the span of a single heartbeat, she considered calling off this little adventure. But just as quickly, she pitched that idea out of her head. She was done with being a coward. These were bones. They could do nothing to her.

Unless there were hyenas lingering around.

She tossed away that thought, too. It was too late to worry about hyenas. If they encountered any, she and Abena would outsmart them, the same way she and Simba had before they had been forced to go back to rescue Zazu.

She had to keep moving forwards, no matter what.

Nala straightened her spine and stuck her chin in the

air, determination settling into *her* bones.

She turned to Abena. "Don't be afraid. I'm right here."

"But… aren't you afraid?"

"No. What do we have to be afraid of? We're lionesses. We're at the top of the food chain."

Abena stood up straight. "You're right," she said with a firm nod. "Lionesses are the bravest there are. My mum says we're even braver than the lions but I should never tell them that."

"She's right," Nala said. "So let us be brave and make it across these Shadowlands."

"Race you to the end," Abena said. And then she took off.

Nala groaned. Why did she keep doing that?

CHAPTER ELEVEN

For the second day in a row, Sarabi was awakened by an ear-piercing scream that echoed throughout their sleeping quarters, the sound reverberating against the cave walls. She leapt to attention, her muscles constricting with the instinct to attack. She would not allow those mangy hyenas to ravage their food stores again. She didn't care what Scar thought of them.

Sarabi started for the cave opening but stopped when she realised the commotion was coming from the innermost part of the cave.

Oh no! The cubs!

An instinct of a different kind – the one to protect their young – took over. She rushed deeper into the cave, preparing to give her life for the sake of her pride's cubs. But her steps came to a halt at the sight of the other lionesses scrambling around the sleeping quarters. There didn't appear to be a hyena in sight.

The pride wasn't under attack?

"What is going on?" Sarabi asked.

"She's gone!" Fayola screamed. "My Abena. She's missing!"

Sarabi's stomach dropped. This was even worse than if the hyenas were attacking them. Had they slunk in under the cover of darkness and snatched the young cub?

"So is Nala," Sefu said.

Nala? No!

She loved all the cubs of their pride, but Nala... Nala was special. Nala was the closest link she had to her Simba, the one cub who had known him better than any other. Sarabi instantly sought out Sarafina, who, along with the other lionesses, had her nose to the floor, searching for a whiff of the two cubs.

Sarabi stiffened her spine. She could not allow her emotions to get the better of her. She needed to take charge of the situation so that they could find their cubs and bring them safely home.

"Where are Thandi and Kito?" Sarabi asked. "They were tasked with keeping watch over the food last night.

They must have seen something."

"Ola and Kamari went to fetch them," Sefu said. "But if they had seen something, they would have told us."

Unless they were in pursuit of whatever had made away with the two cubs and didn't have time to come back and alert the rest of the pride.

But Sarabi knew that wasn't the case when the two lionesses appeared a moment later, both panting from the exertion of their run and looking as confused as everyone else.

"Kamari said that Abena and Nala are missing," Thandi said. "When was this discovered?"

"I woke at daybreak, as usual," Fayola said. "Abena wasn't where she usually sleeps."

"Neither was Nala," Sarafina said, her voice hoarse with worry.

Sarabi caught the barest glimpse of the panic in her eyes, but it was all she needed to glean how frightened she was. A few hours ago she could not bear even looking at her friend; just the thought of Sarafina brought forth a rage unlike any Sarabi had experienced in months.

But right now her heart ached for her. She knew better than any of the lionesses the sheer terror that came with learning that your cub was in danger.

Sarabi pushed aside both her hurt for Sarafina and

the pain of losing Simba. She had to keep her focus on the missing cubs. Abena's and Nala's safety was all that mattered.

"We are sure both were in the cave last night?" Sarabi asked, but then she realised how foolish it was to even present such a question. Sarafina barely let Nala out of her sight these days; of course she was sure her daughter was in the cave last night.

Which made the cubs' disappearance all the more puzzling. There had to be an explanation.

"Could the hyenas have made away with them without any of us knowing?" Sefu asked, voicing what none of the others seemed to want to ask.

Although the hyenas were not known for their self-discipline, they could be stealthy when the occasion warranted. It was yet another reason Sarabi did not trust them and wanted them off her land.

"No," Thandi and Kito said at the same time. "We patrolled Pride Rock throughout the night. We would have spotted a hyena."

"Well, they could not have simply vanished!" Fayola screamed. "*Some*thing happened to them. You and Kito should have done a better job of keeping watch."

Thandi ran up to Fayola and growled at her. "We did our job."

"Not if the hyenas snatched my girl!"

Fayola had become hysterical, while Sarafina seemed to be just the opposite. She stood against the wall of the cave, staring unseeingly at the floor.

"Enough of this!" Sarabi shouted. "None of this back-and-forth will help us find the cubs. We must go in search of them." She looked to Thandi. "You and Sefu, go to the water hole."

"Someone needs to question the hyenas."

"No," Sarabi said. "That is against the king's rule. We are not to question the hyenas." The words tasted foul on her tongue, but Scar had established a set of laws when it came to life between the lionesses and the hyenas. The interlopers he'd allowed to inhabit Pride Rock were not to be approached by any of the lionesses.

"Kito, you and I will go to Scar," Sarabi said. "He is the reason the hyenas are here, so he should be the one to answer for them."

"I will—" Fayola began, but Sarabi cut her off.

"You will stay here with the other cubs."

"I cannot, Sarabi. Do not order me to remain here while my Abena is out there somewhere."

"Fayola, you are in no condition to search for her. You will do more harm than good. Stay here and watch over the other cubs." Sarabi looked to Sarafina. "And her," she said, nodding towards her friend, who continued to stare at the floor.

It was then that Sarabi realised that spot was likely where Nala had been sleeping. The tightness returned to her chest. She wasn't sure which was worse – to lose a cub the way she had lost Simba, when she'd had no ability to save him, or to have a cub snatched right from under your nose. She ached to comfort her friend.

But right now Sarafina needed her action more than she needed her comfort.

"Let's go," Sarabi said to her sister. Thandi and Sefu had already taken off for the water hole, so Sarabi led Kito out of the cave and raced up to the top of Pride Rock to Scar's sleeping quarters.

"Come out, Scar," Sarabi called. Her summons was met with silence. She would give him only a few seconds more before she went into the cave to get him.

"Scar!"

Zazu flew out of the cave and landed in front of her. "Queen Sarabi! Well, this is a pleasant surprise. What are you doing up here?"

"Zazu, where is Scar?"

The bird tipped his head to the side. "I believe he went for his morning exercise. His… uh… *Majesty*" – Zazu spat on the ground after saying the word – "likes to run along the southern edge of the Pride Lands."

Sarabi looked to Kito. "That's where we will go."

"What is going on, Your Majesty?" Zazu asked.

"Zazu, I need you to do a sweep of the area. Two of the cubs are missing. Maybe you can spot them from above."

"Missing?" he gasped.

"Yes. Go," Sarabi said. "We do not know if they were taken or if they left on their own. All we know is that it happened sometime during the night."

"They wouldn't have left on their own," Kito said. "Especially not Sarafina's girl."

Sarabi wasn't so sure about that. It seemed much of the pride had forgotten how independent Nala used to be, back before her mother had begun to smother her.

"We cannot rule out anything," Sarabi said.

"The hyenas have posed a threat to the cubs from the moment they arrived at Pride Rock. They are responsible for this," Kito said.

Sarabi feared her sister was right, which was why she needed to confront Scar as soon as possible.

She and Kito started for the southern edge of the Pride Lands, keeping their eyes open for Nala and Abena as they searched for Scar. They did not catch a whiff of the cubs or their king.

Scar. Not *her* king, but Scar.

She referred to him as *king* when speaking to the other lionesses, because that was the law by which they lived. But she had vowed never to *think* of him as her king. She had but one king.

How she wished she could talk to him. She needed Mufasa's wisdom and his steady paw. Their entire pride needed his leadership right now.

But Mufasa was not here, so she would need to step into his paw prints.

You can do this. You're strong.

"Is it possible Scar already made his way back to Pride Rock?" Kito asked, huffing from the exertion of their exhausting run. The sun had risen high enough in the sky to spread its heat across the savanna. It made their search even more difficult.

"It's possible," Sarabi answered. "Let's go back. I also want to check on Sarafina, Fayola and the other cubs."

They retraced their steps, heading back to Pride Rock. But they were intercepted by Thandi before they reached their home.

"Come to the water hole. We found something," Thandi said.

Sarabi made quick work of getting to the water hole, where she found Sefu waiting next to a muddy puddle.

"Here," Sefu said. "We found two sets of paw prints

that can only be the cubs, but the trail stops here."

She pointed her nose at the blend of prints.

From what Sarabi could make out, there were zebras, elephants, hogs and some other animals that had likely shown up at the water hole sometime during the night or early morning. She put her nose to the ground, trying to pick up the cubs' scent. Nothing.

"We tried to sniff them out," Sefu said. "Between the other animals and the muddy ground, I cannot pick up a scent. Maybe Fayola or Sarafina would have better luck."

"What did Scar say?" Thandi asked.

"We haven't talked to him yet," Sarabi said. She started to explain further but stopped as she caught a whiff of something in the air. Sarabi held up a paw and walked towards the short shrubs at the perimeter of the clearing. She sniffed the wet earth.

Was it Nala she smelt or just her memory playing tricks on her? It was something she'd had to contend with for months after losing Simba. She would smell his scent, hear his voice, feel his soft head underneath her chin. She could not be certain whether anything was real or just her imagination.

But Sarabi was sure of one thing. She sniffed at the sky.

"There is more rain on the way," she said. She looked to the east, where thunderous clouds loomed high above them. They would roll in soon enough, and when they unburdened themselves, it would wreak havoc on whatever happened to be underneath them.

She looked to her fellow lionesses. "If Nala and Abena are out there somewhere, I hope they are safe from the storm that is brewing."

CHAPTER TWELVE

"Are we almost there yet?"

Nala did her best not to growl as they continued to claw their way up the steep embankment. If Abena asked her one more time, she just might scream.

"No," she answered. "I warned you this wouldn't be easy when you begged to follow me."

"You didn't warn me enough," Abena said. "So it's your fault."

Nala glared back at her, then had to scramble to reclaim her grip on the crumbly rock.

"Just keep climbing," she told Abena. She looked up at the sky. It was dark even though daylight had arrived some time ago. She had not seen such ominous clouds rolling in over the savanna since she was a tiny cub. "Once we reach the top, we'll need to find shelter and rest for a bit."

"And eat?" Abena asked.

Nala pretended she hadn't heard her. She was hungry too, but she still had not figured out that part of her plan. She knew enough about pouncing to catch a small rodent, but that wouldn't be enough for both her and Abena.

Why had she allowed the cub to follow her?

She knew why, even if she didn't want to admit it.

Abena was annoying and could not go more than a few minutes without asking a question, but Nala had been grateful to have her by her side as she'd made her way through this Elephant Graveyard. If she was being honest, she could admit that the cub's incessant talking had been useful at times. Answering her many, many, *many* questions had given Nala something else to focus on instead of the creepiness of the Shadowlands.

Not for the first time, Nala questioned the wisdom of making this journey without the aid of an older, more experienced lioness. This was no place for two cubs, especially a cub as young as Abena. Why hadn't she thought to share her suspicions with Sefu? The lioness would have probably joined Nala on her quest to find Simba.

No. If she had told Sefu, then the lioness would have felt compelled to share Nala's knowledge about Garamba with Sarabi. Their queen would have dispatched a cadre of lionesses, but Nala would not have been part of their group. She would have been stuck at Pride Rock, under her mother's paw. As usual.

This was *her* journey, no one else's. She had to show her pride that she could do this. Until she proved to her mother and all the others what she was truly capable of, they would continue to treat her like a baby. She could not allow that to happen.

"I think we're almost there," Nala said. "I can see grass."

She grasped at another rock and started to heave herself up.

Suddenly the rock gave way.

"Not again!" Nala screeched as she went sliding. She grimaced as something ripped into her skin, the searing pain making her see stars. Nala shuddered at the thought of having to make this treacherous climb again, but then something solid stopped her downward slide.

"I've got you!"

It was Abena. Well, it was Abena's head. The cub had bent her head in a way that provided a ledge for Nala to balance on.

"Wait. Let me grab hold of this rock," Nala said. She stretched as far as she could, using her claws to grip the rough surface. With another heave, she was off

Abena's head and back on track.

Nala clawed her way up until she reached the grassy ledge. She turned and immediately dropped to her belly, reaching down so that she could grab on to Abena and help her up. Her side still burned, but she did her best to ignore the pain.

"Come on," Nala said. She repeated the cub's words back to her. "I've got you."

Nala grasped her paw and, with a mighty roar, heaved the smaller cub up and onto the ledge.

"We did it!" Abena cheered. "We made it!"

"Yes, we did," Nala said. She looked back towards the murky bowl of skeletons and geysers they'd just traversed. She and Simba hadn't made it nearly this far before Mufasa had rescued them from a fate that was so scary it made her shiver even to this day.

Nala looked at Abena and smiled. "We made it! We really made it through the Elephant Graveyard! There's nothing to stop me now. I'm going to get to Garamba."

Abena frowned. "What's a garamba?"

Nala's muscles tensed. How could she have been so careless?

"Wait, isn't that the jungle?" Abena asked. "I heard Ola talk about it. She said it's supposed to be very pretty." Abena's eyes brightened. "Is that where we're going?"

Nala didn't know what to say. No one was supposed to know her true destination. But, then again, Abena had just possibly saved her life, or at least saved her from rolling to the pit of the Elephant Graveyard. And she had proved to be a trusty companion – when she wasn't talking Nala's head off. The least she could do was let her know where they were going. It didn't mean she had to tell her the reason they were going there.

"Yes, we're going to Garamba," Nala said.

The cub had not mentioned Simba, which meant she had not heard the chatter swirling around the water hole about the sighting.

"Why didn't you say that from the very beginning!" Abena said. "That sounds like the perfect adventure! Let's go!"

She took off again, but not before Nala stopped her, catching her by the tail.

"Not so fast," Nala said. "First you have to stop running off. We're beyond the Pride Lands now. The closer we get to the jungle, the easier it will be for me to lose sight of you. We have to stick near each other."

"And second?" Abena asked.

"We have to find a river or a water hole," Nala said.

"And food. I'm hungry."

Nala had paid attention to the position of the bull-shaped

cluster of stars before the sun had made them impossible to see. She was pretty sure if they continued straight, they would remain on the right path. But to be safe, she planned to slow their forward progress just a bit. It was smarter to pick up the pace at night, while they had the stars to guide them, and eat and rest during the day.

Now to find food.

Abena gasped. "What happened to you?"

Nala looked down at where the cub stared and finally saw the cause of the stinging. A gash stretched down her side. The fur around it was caked with blood and dirt.

"I think it was a rock," Nala said. "It happened when I lost my footing and started sliding."

Seeing the cut made her aware of how much it actually hurt. She thought about how much worse it could have been if Abena had not halted her tumble, and she felt an overwhelming sense of gratitude towards the cub.

"Thanks for stopping my fall," Nala told her. Who knows what would have happened if she had been out here alone? She could have very well perished in the pit of that abandoned graveyard. "And, if I haven't said it already, I'm… well… I'm sort of happy you're here."

Abena beamed. "I'm happy I'm here too."

The vegetation thickened now that they'd passed

through the desolate Shadowlands. Nala knew they had not yet hit the jungle – based on the stories she'd heard, the jungles nearing Garamba were so thick and lush that the sun could barely make it through the dense trees. But compared to the savanna, the transitional area they now found themselves in was as close to the jungle as she had ever seen.

Thick ropey vines hung from tall trees, and the grass, though sparse in some places, was twice as high as both her and Abena.

"Nala, look!" Abena said. "A water hole."

They raced over to the water hole. It was tiny compared to the one near Pride Rock, but Nala wasn't going to complain. She lapped at the water, savouring its coolness as it slid down her throat.

She took a tentative step forwards into it, being careful not to slip. Then she submerged herself up to her chin, hissing when the water made contact with the scrape on her side. But then the stinging dulled, replaced by a throb that was still unpleasant but better than before.

"Psst... Nala," Abena whispered. "Over there." Nala looked to where the young cub gestured. Two dik-diks were grazing on a patch of grass, their tiny horns and ears pointing upwards. "We can corner them," Abena said.

A wave of panic crashed over her, but Nala did her

best to curb it. She could do this. The dik-diks were small; they should be easy enough to capture.

"Okay," Nala whispered back, climbing out of the water.

A nervous energy swelled in her bloodstream as she dropped low to the ground and crept towards the two dwarf antelope. Slow and steady. She might not know much when it came to hunting, but she knew a slow-and-steady approach was key to gaining the upper paw on her prey. She also knew that one wrong move – even a slight one – could ruin an entire hunt, which was why her heart pounded in her chest.

Stay calm, Nala chastised.

She peered over at Abena and noticed the look of concentration on the young cub's face. All her focus was directed at the dik-diks. How could she remain so composed and in control? It made Nala even more unsure of herself.

As they approached the dik-diks, Abena motioned with her head. Nala followed her cue and pounced…

And sent the dik-diks scampering away.

"Nala!" Abena shouted. "Why did you do that?"

"You said to go!"

"This" – she nudged her head the way she had a moment ago – "means to go around the other side. Not pounce. You're supposed to approach the dik-diks from the back. You can't just jump right in front of them. They're too quick for that."

"Well, I didn't know!" Nala said. She shook her head and in a defeated whisper, repeated, "I didn't know."

Abena tilted her head to the side, her brow furrowed. "You really *didn't* know what to do, did you?"

"No," Nala said. "All I've learnt so far about hunting is how to pounce, and I don't know everything there is to know about that either. I don't know *when* to pounce, or when I should hold back. And hunting is about more than just pouncing. I don't know the best angle to approach prey, and if I ever catch one, what should I do to subdue it? I haven't learnt any of that."

"I can teach you," Abena said in a soft voice.

Nala was taken aback by the offer, and the pity she saw on the young cub's face made her feel even worse. Abena should have been coming to *her* for advice, not the other way around.

But she knew when to shut up and swallow her pride.

"Are you sure?" Nala asked.

"I don't know everything, but my ma let me join her and Ola on a couple of hunts. I can teach you what I learnt from them."

Her first instinct was to feel resentful, but it was quickly followed by gratitude.

Nala nodded. "I'd like that."

They found a shrub that, if she tilted her head to the

side and squinted, Nala could almost imagine was a yellow mongoose. For the next hour, Abena shared tips on how to stalk and capture prey. She was not the most patient teacher, dramatically falling to the ground and wailing at the tiniest mistake, but she didn't give up on her student.

And Nala refused to quit on herself. She could feel her confidence growing.

"Shhh…" Abena said, crouching low. Nala did the same and took aim at the shrub.

"No, no," Abena whispered. "Over there."

Nala whipped around. She spotted a hare standing near the water hole, nibbling on a piece of fruit.

"Do you think you're ready to catch it?" Abena asked.

Instant panic filled Nala's chest, but she tamped it down and nodded. She could do this. She just had to do all the things Abena had taught her.

She took a step forwards, and the hare stood up straight. Nala paused with her paw suspended above the ground, waiting for the hare's next move. She watched as it sniffed the air and looked around. She held herself rigid, pulling in slow, quiet breaths.

When the hare went back to eating its fruit, Nala made her move. She crept closer, using the taller grass for cover. She stopped at the end of the grassy barrier, the hare mere yards away. Nala hunched low, her hind legs bent and in position to spring her forwards. She shot out, aiming for the hare.

It escaped before she could grab hold of it.

Nala didn't know if she wanted to growl or cry. She had done everything right. How had the hare managed to get away? Had it heard her? Was she breathing too hard? Had she pounced too slowly?

"It isn't your fault, you know," Abena said, coming up beside her. "It takes practice."

Nala tried not to feel defeated. Abena was right; it *did* take practice. This was why the lionesses started taking cubs on hunts when they were still very young. If that wildebeest stampede had never happened – if Simba were still at Pride Rock and things were as they should be – Nala would be hunting baby antelope, aardvarks and maybe even caracals.

She *had* to find Simba and bring him back.

If he was still alive, that is.

Nala had known even before she set out on this mission that it was very likely the lion spotted in Garamba was not Simba, but the tiny chance that it was him kept her going.

"I'm sorry I couldn't catch the hare," Nala said to Abena. "I know you're hungry."

"That's okay. I saw another one on the other side of the water hole," she said. She headed off in that direction. When Nala started to follow, Abena put her paw on her shoulder and said, "Let me do this."

Nala jerked her head back, beyond offended that the young cub didn't think she could provide at least *some* help. But when Abena returned just a short time later carrying a dead hare between her teeth, Nala was hard-pressed to hold on to her outrage.

The hare wasn't very big, but it was enough to provide sustenance for both of them.

"Thanks for this," Nala said as she finished up the last bites of food.

"It's no problem," Abena said. "I like hunting. I can't wait until I'm big enough to go on hunts with Ola, Lindiwe and all the others. They always come back with the best stories."

"Yeah, I know," Nala said.

She had suffered through enough of their stories to know exactly what she was missing out on. Not only was she not learning basic skills she desperately needed to survive, but she was also missing out on developing the close friendships it took to feel as if one were truly a member of the pride. Her own mother shared that sisterhood with the older lionesses, yet it didn't seem to matter to her that Nala was quickly becoming an outcast amongst her peers.

"It's too bad your mum thinks you're still a baby," Abena said.

"She does not," Nala lied.

"That's what Ola and Kahina both say. It's okay. My mum thinks I'm still a baby too."

"But you *are* a baby."

"I am not!" Abena said.

"You're younger than I am," Nala pointed out.

"It doesn't mean I'm a baby. I hunt better than you do."

She had her there. But just because the younger cub was a better hunter, it didn't mean she and Nala were equals.

"You're still a baby compared to me," Nala said with a shrug. "As a junior cub, I have to answer to the older lionesses like Sefu and Kito, and they have to answer to the lionesses who have been around even longer than they have, like Thandi and your mother. And they all have to answer to Sarabi. As the youngest member of the pride, you have to answer to… well… everyone. That's just the way things are."

"Well, I don't like it," Abena said. "It's not my fault that I'm the youngest member of the pride. It's not fair." Abena huffed and turned. She began marching back towards the small water hole.

"Don't get mad," Nala called. "You won't be the youngest for long. Olee will have her cub soon."

"It's not fair!" was Abena's reply. She continued her march, indignantly stomping… right into a mud pit.

Nala raced to the puddle. It was the size of a hippo. The grass surrounding it was so high that she had not seen this muddy hazard lurking either.

Nala giggled as Abena flailed around, slipping and sliding as she tried to gain purchase. She reached out a paw, but the young cub turned her nose up at it.

"No," Abena said. "I don't need your help. I'll get out on my own."

"Fine." Nala shrugged and sat back on her hind legs, preparing to enjoy the show. But then she heard a low rumble, and a moment later she felt a tremor underfoot.

"What is that?" Abena asked.

"Shhh…" Nala said.

The sound grew louder and the earth began to shake in earnest. Nala looked to Abena, whose eyes were wide. It seemed to register with the cub at the same time it did with Nala.

They both screamed, "Elephant stampede!"

CHAPTER THIRTEEN

Terror pumped through Nala's heart as she dived into the water-filled pit and scrambled after Abena. She skidded on the slippery sludge, tumbling face-first into the mud.

"Nala, help me!" Abena screamed.

Panic surged within Nala as the violent thumping of heavy footfalls pounding the ground grew louder.

They had to get out. Now. If they didn't, it would mean certain death, for both her and Abena.

Nala pushed herself up and immediately sank back down into the mud. The pounding grew louder. The mud rippled like the surface of the water hole when a bird dropped a rock in its centre. She could feel the ground vibrating, the rumble becoming more intense with every second that passed.

Nala peered over her shoulder. It would only take two steps to make it back to dry ground, but she refused to leave without Abena. Even if it meant her own demise.

But that wasn't going to happen either. She would get them out of this. She refused to allow a stampede to rob their pride of two more members.

By sheer force of will, Nala steadied herself on all fours and crawled through the thick mud until she reached Abena.

She clamped the cub's scruff between her teeth and pulled.

Come on. Come on. Come on.

With one last pull, Nala heaved Abena out of the muck and onto more stable land.

She'd done it. She'd actually done it.

"We have to get out of here!" Abena screamed, knocking Nala out of her shocked daze.

"This way!" Nala yelled, and ushered Abena ahead of her, nudging the cub's hindquarters with her head before they both took off for the closest tree. Nala glanced to her right. Her eyes widened at the pack of elephants charging towards them at full speed.

"Climb! Climb! Climb!" she yelled. "Get to that thick branch and hold on tight."

Nala made it to the branch just after Abena, right as the first elephant stormed past the tree. She wrapped her forelegs around Abena, who was firmly holding on to the branch.

"I've got you," Nala shouted into her ear. "Just keep holding it tight."

The tree canted from side to side, leaning so far towards the ground that Nala feared they had not climbed high enough. As if the swaying wasn't bad enough, the tree shook like the elephants were trying to wiggle marula fruit free from the branches. If either of them let go for even a second, they would go tumbling to the ground.

The stampede seemed to go on forever though it lasted only a few minutes. As far as Nala could tell, there were only about two dozen elephants in total.

Unbidden, Scar's description of the wildebeest stampede that had killed Mufasa popped up in her mind. She could scarcely imagine the devastation thousands and thousands of animal hooves left behind. Overwhelming anguish ripped through her at the thought of what their king had faced that horrible day.

And Simba.

Please, please, let him be alive. Let him have not gone through such terrible pain.

"Do you think it's safe to climb down?" Abena asked from underneath her.

"What?" Nala blinked several times, Abena's inquiry knocking her out of her uncomfortable memories of the past and back into the present. "We should be safe now that they've passed, but let me make sure everything is okay."

She lifted her head and surveyed the land around them to ensure there were no stragglers that had fallen behind the stampede. She saw no elephants and only a few other animals off in the distance. Based on the shape of their horns, it looked like a family of kudus.

"All appears to be safe," Nala said.

She led the way down the tree, taking in the difference in the texture of the ground following the stampede. The elephants had kicked up mud and pulverised rocks into dust. Another chill ran through her when she thought of what would have happened had she and Abena been too far away from the tree or if they had stayed stuck in that mud for just a minute longer. They would have been crushed, never to be heard from again.

But that *hadn't* happened. Because *she* had saved them both! She had really done it!

Sure, she had panicked for a moment, but then she'd pushed her fear aside and got the job done. How she wished her mother had been here to witness it all.

"That was scary," Abena said. "I didn't know elephants could run so fast."

"Anything can run fast if you give it a good reason to," Nala said.

"Even hippopotamuses?"

She nodded. "Some hippos can run as fast as elephants."

The dust the elephants had stirred up with their stampede began to settle, but something eerie still hung in the air. Nala looked up at the sky. The white clouds that had hovered above them had turned dark grey. They were also much closer, so close it felt as if she would be able to reach up and grab one if she were but a little taller.

A fat raindrop landed on her nose.

She blinked several times in confusion. She had missed yesterday's brief storm, only seeing the results of it as she and Abena travelled across the clearing and grasslands during their escape from Pride Rock. The dry season had lasted so long that she had forgotten what rain felt like, but as the thick raindrops began to tumble with fierce speed from the heavy clouds, Nala could tell this was different from a typical rainstorm. She had heard the elder lionesses speak of the wet seasons of the past, and how unpredictable the weather had become in more recent years.

The rain began to fall harder, and a loud crack of thunder rent the air.

"We need to find shelter," Nala called to Abena. "I noticed a kopje while we were up in the tree. Hopefully, we can reach it before the storm gets too bad."

Nala led the way, heading for the small hill she'd

spotted. This part of the savanna remained flat but it was speckled with kopjes, rock formations that were smaller than Pride Rock but still sufficient for shelter. The kopje she had seen appeared to have trees they could hide under, but she was hoping there was an overhang that could provide even better protection.

By the time she and Abena arrived at the kopje, the rain was coming down so hard Nala could barely make out the hill. She slipped several times as she scaled its rocks, made slicker by the pummelling rain.

"Over there," she called, pointing to a large boulder with a flat surface. Another rock hung over it, offering a shield from the relentless rain.

Nala noticed something scurry from the area. She figured it was a rodent, or a pygmy fox, or some other creature that could possibly have been a meal, but food was not a priority at the moment. Staying safely out of this fierce storm was the only thing she cared about right now.

Once she and Abena reached the tiny alcove, they moved as far away from the opening as they could.

A bright light flashed in the sky, followed by frighteningly loud thunder that seemed to roll on and on for the longest time.

"I'm scared," Abena said, burying her face against Nala's chest. Nala rocked gently back and forth, remembering how good that always made her feel when her mother would do the same with her.

Despite the strain that had stretched between Nala and her mother lately, a fierce longing for her mother's embrace slammed into Nala. Nothing felt safer than being surrounded by her solid strength, her tongue issuing comforting licks to the top of Nala's head.

The moments she'd experienced with Abena today had given her a glimpse into the responsibility her mother must have felt to keep Nala safe. The fear she'd suffered while trying desperately to tug Abena out of the mud pit before the elephants arrived, to protect her while up in that tree, was all-consuming. In those moments, making sure the young cub was safe was the only thing that mattered.

Guilt rushed through Nala with the fierceness of an overflowing river at the realisation of how worried her mother must be right now.

I'm okay, Mama.

Maybe if she concentrated on the words hard enough, her mother would somehow feel them.

The rain and thunder continued to batter them. Nala held on to Abena, for both the cub's sake and her own. Until finally, after what seemed like a lifetime, the rain began to taper off and the heavy grey clouds drifted past them, ushering in the bright sun.

Abena's tiny body still shook.

"Nala?" The cub said.

"Hmm?"

"I don't want to go on an adventure anymore."

Nala jerked her head back. "What?"

"This is too scary. I want to go back home."

"We can't go back," she argued.

"Yes, we can," Abena said. "We just have to walk through that Elephant Graveyard, and the scrubland, and then we're back at Pride Rock. Please, Nala. I don't want to go to Garamba."

Nala wanted to scream. She *knew* she never should have allowed the cub to follow her. She should have predicted this. Abena was nothing but a baby. She wasn't ready for a journey of this magnitude.

"I'm going to Garamba. You can return to Pride Rock if you want to," Nala said.

Abena looked up at her with frightened wide eyes. "By myself?"

"I will lose an entire day if I have to take you back," Nala said.

Abena's eyes filled with tears.

Nala threw her head back and growled, because she knew there was no way she could allow the cub to return to Pride Rock on her own. Chances were high that

Abena would get lost before she ever made it through the Shadowlands. *If* she made it through the Shadowlands. She would probably get eaten by a cheetah or a hyena or any number of animals just waiting to sink their teeth into a plump lion cub.

"I'm sorry," Abena said. "I just want to go home. Please, just take me home."

Nala released a frustrated sigh. She knew what she had to do.

CHAPTER FOURTEEN

Scar frowned as he felt the warmth of the sun fade from his face. He twisted atop his favourite rock, the smooth, flat one near the pinnacle of Pride Rock. He'd coveted this exact rock for years. It was perfect for the long naps he preferred to take; he could bathe in the sun and while away the hours until the lionesses brought him his food.

But there was no whiling away in the sun because the sun was no longer shining.

Scar lifted one lazy eyelid and peered up at the sky. Those clouds looked ominous. They would ruin his day.

"Oh, phooey," he said. "I ask for one simple nap in the sun, and I cannot even get that. What's good about being king if the universe will not cooperate in granting my every wish?"

Although he should not complain. The dry season had lasted much too long. He would never admit it to her, but Sarabi had been right when she spoke of it playing a part in the scarcity of food. Maybe the impending rain would be enough to encourage vegetation to start growing again and bring back some of those plant eaters that served as such wonderful meals for him and his ilk.

Scar's frown deepened as the faint sounds of a commotion rose up from somewhere below. Apparently, no one wanted him to get any rest today.

He dragged himself from his lounging rock and walked over to the ledge so that he could peer down at the clearing. The lionesses were frantic in their movements, running around like his hyena friends were chasing their young again.

Please, say it wasn't so. He'd warned the hyenas to stay away. He didn't need the headache. But he didn't see any of the hyenas, so it couldn't be that.

Scar narrowed his eyes, zeroing in on Sarabi, who seemed to have taken charge, as usual.

Were they plotting a takeover?

He had spent the last six months anticipating the hour they would turn on him. Their bitterness hung over Pride Rock, permeating the air with the stench of resentment. Scar knew without a doubt that, if given the chance, they would banish him from this throne that was rightfully his.

He bared his teeth, unable to withhold his angry growl as he watched them plotting his demise.

It wasn't supposed to be this way. The lionesses should have fallen in line; it was what happened when a new leader stepped in to command a pride.

Maybe he was jumping to conclusions. Sarabi and her lionesses had never outright defied him; it's just that they didn't show enough… enthusiasm. He wanted their adoration, or at the very least, their respect.

He would have his little stooge find out what had caused the ruckus amongst them.

"Zazu?" Scar called.

He waited for the bird to respond. When he didn't, Scar turned and peered around the landing. It only now occurred to him that he had not seen Zazu since he returned from his morning exercise. Where was that dodo bird?

"Zazu?" Scar called again, his anger rising.

He put up with more disrespect from that bird than he should, but this was beyond the pale. Scar knew for a fact that Mufasa had never had to call for the little pea-brained fowl more than once. The moment his brother opened his mouth, Zazu was there, ready to grant his every wish. Scar expected the same deference.

"ZAZU!"

A moment later, the bird swooped in from the north, landing at Scar's feet.

"Yes, Sire?" he asked. He was winded, and his feathers looked ruffled as if he were agitated.

"Where were you?" Scar asked.

"I… I was ordered by Queen Sarabi—"

"*I* am your king," Scar hissed. "You do not take orders from Sarabi." He pressed his nose to the bird's beak and growled. "We have been over this before, Zazu. You are *my* majordomo. Not Sarabi's, but *mine!*"

"Yes, Sire," Zazu said.

Scar backed away, satisfied by the abject fright he saw in the bird's eyes.

"Now that we have that taken care of, I want you to fly down to the clearing and find out what has the lionesses in an uproar. I can hear them from all the way up here."

"Oh, oh, Sire, I do not have to fly down to the clearing to figure that out. I already know. That is why Queen… uh…"

"Out with it," Scar said between clenched teeth.

"Two of the cubs have gone missing," Zazu said. "The lionesses have been searching for them all morning. I, myself, flew above half of the Pride Lands, but I found no trace of them."

"Is that so?" Scar said.

He began a slow stroll around the landing. Now that he

knew the lionesses were not down there conspiring to get rid of him, he wasn't as interested in their little palaver.

"Sire, did you hear me? Two of the cubs are missing. Are you not concerned?"

Hmm... now that he thought about it, maybe he *should* show some concern. Even if he wasn't. It was what Mufasa would do.

Not that he wanted to emulate his brother in any way. This was *his* pride and he ruled it the way he saw fit. But Scar had to admit that it would be nice if he could finally win over the lionesses. Maybe showing that he cared about their little smelly cubs would gain points in his favour.

"Of course I am concerned," Scar said. "I must go down there at once."

Scar started down Pride Rock. He quickly realised that a truly concerned king would make haste, so he picked up the pace, reaching the clearing in record time.

The lionesses all stopped what they were doing when he entered their space.

"What is this I hear about missing cubs?" Scar asked.

Sarabi started to speak, but it was Fayola who ran up to him, getting in his face.

"They took my Abena!" the lioness shouted at him. "It's those hyenas! I know it is! You brought them here!"

Scar growled at the lioness. He should have her

banished from the pride for her outburst.

"Fayola, please," Sarabi said.

Two of the other lionesses closed in on her, dragging her away. Scar stared her down.

"I will not accept such disrespect," Scar said, turning to Mufasa's widow. "Tell me what has happened?"

"When Fayola awakened this morning, she discovered her daughter Abena and Sarafina's daughter, Nala, were missing. We have been searching all day and have covered a large swath of the Pride Lands, but we cannot find them." Sarabi stuck her nose in the air. "I am starting to suspect that the hyenas have taken them."

Twin cries rang out from the lionesses gathered close by. Scar glanced over and saw the two who were being comforted, Fayola and Sarafina. It occurred to him that Sarafina's girl was the one who had always been with Simba.

"The hyenas know that they are not to disturb the lionesses," Scar said. "I have warned them."

"Maybe they decided not to heed your warning," Sarabi said.

His eyes shot back to her, but he managed not to lash out. He must maintain control. He should be showing concern, not irritation at these insolent members of his pride.

"The hyenas obey my command. They know that it is a condition of their remaining here at Pride Rock," Scar said.

"However, I shall question them about it. Maybe they heard something during the night."

Gratitude flashed across Sarabi's face.

Well, that was interesting. Scar wondered what it would take to turn that gratitude into admiration. Or, better yet, reverence.

That is what he wanted from the members of his pride. He wanted the same respect and devotion they'd shown to Mufasa for so many years, and this was the first time he had seen even a hint of it. Maybe he had been wrong in his approach these last six months.

"Leave this to me," Scar said. "I promise, if those hyenas had anything to do with this, they will pay a high price."

Sarabi nodded. "Thank you, Scar."

He left them in the clearing and made his way to the area of Pride Rock where the hyenas resided, in the shadow of the rock formation.

"That is very good of you, Sire. Surely, the lionesses appreciate your taking command in this way," Zazu said, flying to the right of him. "Reminds me of Mufasa."

Scar whipped his tail at the bird. "Go back to the lionesses," he said.

He didn't need anyone comparing him to his brother. And he didn't need that bird sticking his beak into his business with the hyenas.

Scar grunted.

He detested that he even had any business with the hyenas. What he wouldn't give to be done with those mangy bottom feeders. But they had shown loyalty to him when his own pride had not, so he would continue to tolerate them. He and the hyenas, they had an… understanding. He would continue to honour it until it no longer suited him. For now, those hyenas still served a purpose.

Scar rounded a boulder and spotted Banzai. At least it wasn't Ed, who irritated Scar to no end. They all irritated him, if he was being honest, but none more than Ed.

Banzai would be of no use to him today. He needed the one who considered herself their leader.

"Shenzi," Scar called. "Come here at once!"

The hyena sauntered out from between the two large rocks she fancied as her headquarters.

"Oh, hey there, Scar," she said. "What brings you down here to hang out with the riff-raff?"

The other hyenas chuckled. Their incessant laughter grated on his nerves. The only thing they seemed to take seriously was their next meal.

"What do you know about missing lion cubs?" Scar asked Shenzi.

Her eyes widened. "We killed that little lion cub, Scar. I told you that months ago. You're the rightful king because Mufasa and his runt are dead."

"I'm not talking about Simba, you fool. I know he is dead. I'm talking about the two lion cubs that went missing last night."

Shenzi's head snapped back. "Last night?"

"Yes, two of the cubs are missing, and Sarabi believes you hyenas may have had something to do with it."

"She's lying on us, Scar," Banzai said. "Don't believe a word she says."

"He's right," Shenzi said. "We stay away from those lionesses." She looked around at the other hyenas and grinned. "Now, the kills they bring in are another matter. That zebra they brought home the other night looked so good, we couldn't stay away."

They all fell over laughing, rolling around on the ground like the idiots they were.

"We will discuss your pillaging the food stores too," Scar said. "But not today. There are more important matters to be concerned about."

Besides, he wasn't up for arguing with these deplorables over their raiding the food. It was the job of the lionesses to hunt. They needed to do a better job of it.

"So, no one here had anything to do with the disappearance of those cubs?" he asked. "I can take your word for it?"

"Absolutely, Scar. It wasn't us. I swear," Shenzi confirmed.

He shrugged.

That was that. He'd done what he'd promised Sarabi and the others he would do. Let them figure out what happened to their cubs. It was no longer his problem.

Besides, it's what they deserved for treating him the way they had since he took over as their leader.

CHAPTER FIFTEEN

Nala swatted at a beetle that buzzed near her ear as she lay at the edge of the grasslands, crouched low. She was trying to be covert here. All she needed was a pesky insect giving away their location.

Although Nala was pretty sure there was no one around to alert. All was calm.

Still, even though they were back on her pride's lands, she was keeping her eyes open for potential predators. This past day of having to be the grown-up had given her a new appreciation for the security the older lionesses provided. She'd never considered the heavy responsibility those watching out for her felt while she had played around carefree, but she would from now on.

"Let's go," Nala whispered to Abena. "Remember, be quiet."

After the rain had finally let up, she and Abena had left the shelter of the kopje. They'd come upon a family of gazelles grazing near the mud pit where Abena had got stuck. Once Nala assured them that they were not there to hunt, the mama gazelle shared with her a quicker way to the Pride Lands, one that bypassed the Elephant Graveyard.

She and Abena had begun the trek back to Pride Rock, making it to the grasslands on the outskirts of their kingdom just as the sun was beginning to set. Now all she had to do was get Abena halfway to the water hole. Nala trusted that the cub would be okay to travel the rest of the way home, and it would give *her* time to put some distance between herself and Pride Rock. Even though she had made Abena swear that she would not give away her location or where she was headed, Nala was taking no chances.

And now that the sun was inching closer to the horizon, the cluster of bull stars would be out again, ready to lead the way to Simba.

It was difficult for Nala to hold in her excitement. When she'd mentioned Garamba to the gazelle, the slim antelope said she and her family had just returned from the Zemongo Faunal region and had passed through Garamba. She had assured Nala that she was on the right track. And, even better, that she should be able to reach Garamba in less than two days.

Knowing she was so close to potentially finding her best friend had renewed her resolve to see this through. She was eager to get back to her journey.

But first, she had to return Abena home safely.

"Come on," Nala said. "Let's get a bit closer."

She looked overhead, searching for Zazu. It would be just her luck that the bird would choose to fly around this area just as she and Abena were returning. But thankfully, the coast remained clear. They didn't encounter Zazu, any of the lionesses from their pride, or any other animal, for that matter. It almost seemed too good to be true.

They reached the smallest of the baobab trees that grew near the perimeter of the grasslands, where they met up with the open savanna. The vegetation was sparse here, with far fewer places to take cover. Nala stopped and turned to Abena.

"Okay, you have to travel the rest of the way on your own," she said.

Panic shot into Abena's eyes, but it was quickly replaced with confidence. She stood up straight and nodded. "I can do it," she said.

Nala begrudgingly admitted to herself that she was

going to miss having the cub by her side. Thanks to her mum, she and Abena had more in common than Nala had first thought – not only did they both resent being treated like babies, but they both hated violent thunderstorms, too.

What had shocked Nala most about Abena was just how strong-willed she was, and smart. She was *so* smart. It wasn't until she'd taken the time to really listen to the cub that Nala realised just how much their pride underestimated their youngest member.

The cub had opened Nala's eyes in multiple ways in the short amount of time since they had taken off together. The brief hunting lesson was the most important thing Nala had learnt, of course, but she'd also learnt how to stand up for herself. Even though Abena was smaller and younger, she had refused to back down when Nala tried to pressure her into following Nala's rules.

Nala used to have that kind of confidence in herself. It had taken this brave little cub to remind her that it was still there, lurking inside of her. She just had to believe she could do this.

"Are you ready?" Nala asked.

Abena nodded.

"Now, you remember what I said, right?"

Another nod. "I will tell the lionesses that I followed you when you sneaked out of the sleeping quarters, but I got lost before I ever made it off the Pride Lands. And then I fell asleep under a jackalberry tree."

"Good," Nala said. Abena had remembered their story. "And don't forget to mention that I am long gone and you don't remember the direction I was heading, so there is no use in anyone looking for me."

"Oh, I forgot the part about the rain," Abena said. "I'll tell them that the rain came and I was too afraid to move, which is why it took so long to make it back to Pride Rock. At least that part is true, so it doesn't feel as if I'm telling a tale to my mama," Abena finished.

Nala hated to lie as well, but she had no choice.

Although what she hated even more than lying was envisioning how worried her mother would be to know that Nala was out here somewhere.

"On second thought, why don't we stick closer to the truth?" Nala said. She started warming up to the idea. "Yeah, you can tell them that we *did* leave the Pride Lands together, but you don't remember how to get back to where we were. However, they shouldn't worry because I am okay. Tell my mother I just wanted to go on an adventure and I will be back home soon. But whatever you do, do *not* mention Garamba," Nala said. "No one can know that I'm going there."

Abena tipped her head to the side. "But I don't

understand why. You told the gazelle that you were going to Garamba."

"That was different," Nala said. "No one from Pride Rock can know. Promise me, Abena. Do not say the word *Garamba*. If you do, you will ruin everything."

"I won't," Abena said. She frowned. "Are you sure you will be okay on your own? How will you eat?"

"I don't have to eat for another day, at least. And, when it's time to find food again, I'll hunt." She playfully bumped Abena with her shoulder. "I had a pretty good teacher give me some tips."

"Are you *sure* you still want to go on your adventure?" Abena asked. "It was scary out there. What if there is another storm?"

"I'll find shelter," Nala said. "Don't worry about me."

"Okay," she said. "And I won't tell anyone where you are going. I promise." She nudged her head against Nala's neck. "Be careful out there, Nala. I hope you have a lot of fun on your adventure." She looked up at her and smiled. "The next time Ola and Kahina call you a coward, I'm going to tell them they don't know what they're talking about. You're one of the bravest cubs I know."

"Thanks," Nala said, her chest growing warm at the young cub's praise. "I'll be back soon. And I may just bring you a surprise. A good one."

A *really* good one. That was her entire reason for doing this, to bring her pride the best surprise they all could ever hope for.

"It's time for you to go." Nala nudged her. "Go on."

Abena nodded, then turned and took off across the grasslands. Nala huddled next to the baobab tree's thick trunk and watched the cub as she travelled across the open plateau. She had decided she would remain here until she could no longer see Abena and then stay just a bit longer, until the last of the sunlight dipped below the horizon. She calculated that Abena should reach the water hole around that same time.

She could make out the very tip of Pride Rock from where she stood, but Nala pushed back the feelings of melancholy. She would not allow her mission to succumb to homesickness. Sure, she missed her pride, and she would give anything to alleviate the worry she knew her mum must be feeling, but getting word of her safety from Abena would take care of her mother's distress.

As for her longing for home? Well, she would let thoughts of what the Pride Lands would feel like once Simba returned and took his rightful place as leader of Pride Rock assuage any wistfulness she felt.

She took one final look in the direction Abena had gone, then turned and raced towards the bull-shaped stars.

And, hopefully, towards Simba.

CHAPTER SIXTEEN

Sarabi slowly paced the length of the landing that jutted out from their sleeping quarters. This walk usually summoned feelings of joy as memories of the many times she and Mufasa had stood at the very tip of the landing, looking out over the land he ruled, would often play in her mind. But there was no joy today, only an agonising worry that escalated with every moment that passed without word from Nala and Abena.

The lionesses had come up here to rest after a long day of searching for the cubs, but Sarabi knew rest was not in her future. There were too many hazards out there. It wasn't safe even for a grown lioness to travel those lands; to know that those two young cubs were possibly out there on their own sickened her.

And that was the more positive of the two scenarios. Sarabi did not want to contemplate the other thing that may have happened to the girls. Scar had assured her that the hyenas had nothing to do with their disappearance. Sarabi could do nothing but take him – and therefore the hyenas – at his word.

It was a difficult task. Scar had never given her reason to distrust him in the past, but ever since he took over as the leader of their pride, Sarabi had seen a side of him that he'd previously hidden from her – from all of them. She found herself questioning every decision he made. It was as if he intentionally made choices that went against all that Mufasa stood for, starting with welcoming the hyenas into their kingdom.

Her head told her that Scar would not knowingly stand with the hyenas if he believed they had brought harm to two cubs of his own pride, but her gut cautioned her to keep a wary eye on her brother-in-law.

Sarabi agitatedly swished her tail along the landing. Her misgivings about Scar should be of little concern right now. All that mattered was getting to the bottom of what had become of Nala and Abena.

She glanced over at Fayola and Sarafina, and her heart twisted in empathising pain. The two lionesses lay with their forelegs entwined, one's head resting against the other's.

Fayola's oldest, Ola, lay tucked under her mother's paw. Sadness hung in the air over all of Pride Rock, but it seemed to emanate from the two lionesses and cub in the corner.

"Sarabi?"

She turned to find Thandi standing just behind her. "What is it?" Sarabi asked.

"We need to do something," Thandi said. "I cannot just sit around. I know we should be resting, but who can rest knowing Nala and Abena are out there? Anything could be happening to them. You have to let us continue our search. We'll rest better once we know the cubs are safe."

Sarabi turned and looked at the others. They all seemed anxious to get going. She knew they wanted to be out there searching the savanna, but she also knew if they did not rest and recuperate, their bodies would give out on them. They wouldn't be of help to Abena, Nala or anyone else if that were to happen.

Her lionesses would not go unless she gave them permission; it was a call she hated to make. She asked herself, *What would Mufasa do?* But if she was hoping for a quick answer, she was in for a rude awakening.

She would have to make this decision on her own.

"Did you question the other cubs?" Sarabi asked. "Did they not see anything?"

Thandi shook her head.

"Are they sure Nala did not mention leaving last night?" Sarabi asked.

"Nala did not share anything with any of the cubs," she said. "They said they do not really talk to Nala because" – she glanced towards Sarafina and whispered – "it's because she keeps her so sheltered. They said it isn't fun to play with Nala because Sarafina is always hovering."

And that was the source of their problem, Sarabi was sure of it.

Since returning to Pride Rock to rest and discuss their next steps, the lionesses had come to the conclusion that, if the hyenas had not snatched the cubs, they must have left of their own volition. And it was more likely that Nala was the one who left, with Abena following. Unless Nala had witnessed Abena taking off and had gone in search of her, but Fayola was adamant that Abena would never do such a thing. She had no reason to want to run.

Nala, on the other paw, did. Sarabi knew how frustrated the cub had become with her mother's overprotectiveness. Asking Sarabi to intervene on her behalf had possibly been Nala's last straw.

But she wouldn't be so careless as to leave the Pride Lands, would she?

"Sarabi, can we continue our search?" Thandi asked. "Please."

Sarabi sighed. She turned and walked back to the edge of the landing, hoping for a sign from Mufasa about what to do.

Just as she was about to turn back to Thandi, she caught something out of the corner of her eye. Sarabi squinted, trying to make out the figure running towards Pride Rock. At first she thought it was a fox or a meerkat. But then the cloud that had passed in front of the moon cleared and illuminated the figure.

Realisation dawned.

"Oh my goodness," Sarabi breathed.

She took off, racing down the side of Pride Rock with a vigour she had not felt in months. She heard Thandi calling her name but did not stop to explain. She immediately heard the pounding of multiple paws behind her as the other lionesses fell in line. Sarabi covered the distance between herself and the cub in record time.

But before she could reach Abena, Fayola flew past her. The mother lioness scooped her cub into her forelegs and went tumbling forwards.

Excited gasps rang out as the other lionesses who had followed came upon them. Sarabi took a step back and ordered the others to do the same. Fayola deserved this time with her daughter.

She surveyed the land, searching for Nala. Surely the

other cub could not be far behind.

Sarafina charged into the clearing, screaming her daughter's name. Excitement and panic made her voice sound shrill.

"Nala! Where's Nala! Nala, come here at once!" Sarafina screamed. "Where is she? Nala!"

That was Sarabi's question too. It appeared Abena had returned alone.

Dread churned in the pit of Sarabi's stomach. Something was wrong. The girls had to have left Pride Rock together – there was no way both had decided to leave on the same night but had done so separately. So why was Abena the only one to return?

"Where's Nala?" Sarafina screeched. She ran up to Abena and Fayola and screamed in the younger cub's face. "Where is my girl?"

Sarabi looked to Kito and Sefu. They understood her command without her having to voice it. But when the lionesses tried to pull her away, Sarafina wrenched out of their grasp.

"No! She needs to tell me where Nala is!" she cried.

Sarabi motioned for Thandi to help Kito and Sefu. Together they gathered a wailing Sarafina and moved several feet away, far enough to prevent Sarafina's hysterical cries from scaring Abena, but close enough to hear what was being said by the cub.

Sarabi spoke quietly. "Fayola, I will need to question her. This is important."

Fayola nodded. She turned Abena so that she faced Sarabi, but she did not let go. Sarabi could not fault her for wanting to hold her baby tight.

"Abena, did you leave here with Nala?" Sarabi asked the cub.

She looked away and nodded.

"When?" Sarabi asked.

"Last night," she answered.

"Did the two of you plan this? Did you know you were going to leave before last night?"

She shook her head. "I couldn't sleep. And I saw Nala leave the cave, so I followed her."

"Where is she?!" Sarafina screamed.

Sarabi's eyes darted to where the lionesses held her back, but then she returned her attention to Abena.

"Why didn't Nala return with you? Did you two lose each other?"

She nodded enthusiastically. "Yes. I followed her, but then I got lost and never made it off the Pride Lands. But then—" She stopped. "Wait," Abena said, her forehead scrunching. "That's wrong. We decided to tell the truth."

Sarabi's pulse quickened. "What is the truth?" she asked. "Where is Nala?"

"I don't know," Abena said. "I... I got scared because of the storm?" She shook her head. "No, I didn't get scared. Yes, I *did* get scared. That's the truth. But... I can't remember," she said.

She buried her face against her mother's neck. It was obvious Nala and the younger cub had cobbled together some story for the girl to report back to them.

"It is very important that you tell me the truth, Abena," Sarabi said. "The real truth. Nala is in grave danger."

"No, she just wanted to go on an adventure. She told me to tell her mama that she is safe. She just... she was tired of being treated like a baby. And me too," Abena said. "That's why I went with her. But I really *did* get scared when the storm came. And the elephants, too. There were so many of them. They made the ground rumble."

My goodness. A stampede. They had faced a stampede.

"Nala just wanted to go on an adventure," Abena said. She called out to where the lionesses held Sarafina. "She was mad because you wouldn't let her hunt. But she's not mad anymore because I taught her how to hunt. She's okay."

Sarabi cautioned a glance at her friend. She saw the devastation in Sarafina's eyes, and for the first time, it seemed as if she was finally recognising the part her actions of the last six months had played in this. She had smothered Nala, so the cub had chosen to break free.

"Where is Nala?" Sarabi asked Abena.

She shook her head. "I can't tell you."

"Abena!" Sarabi, Fayola and several of the other lionesses yelled simultaneously.

The cub gasped and buried her face against her mother, but Fayola would not allow her to stay hidden. The time for coddling was over.

"Where did Nala go?" Fayola asked her daughter. "Tell us now, Abena. This is not the time to play around."

"Nala will be so mad at me," she said.

"That does not matter. We need to make sure Nala is safe! We must find her and bring her back to Pride Rock before something horrible happens to her. Now tell us where she was headed."

The cub bowed her head and muttered something unintelligible.

"What was that?" Sarabi asked.

Abena looked up at her and said in a stronger voice, "Garamba."

"Garamba?" Sarafina asked.

"What does she know of Garamba?" Thandi added.

But Sarabi knew.

"She is going after Simba." She closed her eyes and

released a deep breath. "She must have overhead when the mongoose reported the sighting there. Which way did you travel?" Sarabi asked Abena. She looked towards the Shadowlands. "Were there skeletons there? And water that shot up from the ground?"

"The Elephant Graveyard," Abena said. She lifted her chin, an air of cockiness in her voice. "I wasn't afraid of that part, even in the dark. Although by the time we made it to the other side of it, the sun had come up."

So they'd made it through the Shadowlands. Sarabi tried to calculate how far Nala would have travelled in the time it took Abena to make a return trip to Pride Rock. She was likely halfway to Garamba by now. Their problem lay in the vastness of the savanna. There were multiple routes to Garamba, and it would be difficult to know which Nala took. Unless…

"Abena, do you remember a gorge?" Sarabi asked.

The cub frowned. "No."

"What about a mountain?" Sarabi asked. "It would have been very tall, with a smaller one right next to it."

"Yes." She nodded. "I remember seeing it while we were in the tree, waiting for the elephants to run past us. It was still far away, though."

"That's okay," Sarabi said. "This is good." It narrowed their search.

If they had gone the way of the mountain and not the gorge, it meant Nala was travelling northwest, through the pass most of the migrating animals took. It was a shorter route to Garamba, but also more dangerous for a cub to travel alone.

"The skeletons and the mountains are all you remember?" Sarabi asked. The more information the cub could provide, the better their chances of tracking Nala down.

"Yeah, that's it," Abena said. "I wasn't scared of the skeletons, but I'm glad we didn't have to go through the Elephant Graveyard on our way back."

Sarabi stood erect. *Our* way back?

"So, Nala followed you back to Pride Rock?" Sarabi asked.

The cub's eyes widened as if she knew she'd just said something she wasn't supposed to share.

"Tell me, Abena," Sarabi ordered. If Nala had accompanied her, there was still a chance they could catch her before she got too far. "Did Nala bring you back to Pride Rock?"

Abena nodded. "She brought me to the edge of the grasslands and said she would stay until I reached the water hole."

That was all Sarabi needed to hear.

"Lionesses! Assemble!" she called. In an instant, they

were all huddled around her. "There is a chance that Nala is still close by. She followed Abena as far as the perimeter of the grasslands and remained there until Abena reached the water hole. She could not have got far. We will fan out and search for her. Get into pairs.

"I will go with Thandi," Sarafina said.

"No," Sarabi told her.

It hurt her to say the word, but certainly not as much as it hurt Sarafina to hear it. Sarabi knew this would only deepen the rift between them, but the lioness was too excitable to join the search. It was just as it had been when they'd first discovered the cubs were missing and Fayola had demanded to go looking for Abena.

"You will be more of a hindrance than a help," Sarabi said.

"You cannot stop me from searching!" Sarafina cried.

"I have made my decision," Sarabi said. "You will not go."

She almost flinched at the spark of hatred that flashed in her best friend's eyes. That hate was directed solely at Sarabi, and it made her heart shatter, the jagged pieces stabbing her with every breath.

"No one is going."

Sarabi whipped around at the pronouncement.

Scar.

CHAPTER SEVENTEEN

Scar took in the shocked faces of the lionesses and could barely contain his delight. It was deliciously invigorating, this power he wielded over them. They could not take a single step without his say-so. It was something they needed to be reminded of on occasion.

And what better occasion was there than this one, when the fate of one of their own hung in the balance? Yet, they could do nothing about it unless he granted his blessing.

As usual, it was his sister-in-law who spoke up.

"You cannot do this, Scar. We *must* go! Nala is out there. The longer we're standing here, the more distance she will put between herself and home. Do not stop us from going after her."

He donned his most superior look as he stared at her.

"I have spoken. None of you are allowed to go after Nala," he reiterated.

Horrified gasps rang out amongst the lionesses. Sarafina wailed while several of the others stared at him with a mixture of dismay and rage.

"*I* will do it," Scar said.

More gasps, these filled more with shock than horror.

"You?" Sarabi asked.

Yes, him. He was as surprised as they were, if he was being honest. But Nala's little disappearing act had provided Scar with the opportunity he had been seeking. This was his chance to prove his worth to his pride.

Sarabi had been quick to accuse the hyenas of snatching the cub, which meant she ultimately blamed *him*. They still viewed him as being more on the side of the hyenas' kingdom than of his own kind. As if anyone could blame him if that were the case. It wasn't, of course. He was on his *own* side, no one else's.

If he had to choose the ideal existence, it would be one where he ruled Pride Rock better than any of those who had come before him. He'd choose an existence where he had the esteem of the entire animal kingdom. Why did these imbeciles not realise this was all about him?

Once again, their commotion that evening had

awakened him from a pleasant sleep. He had come down to the clearing ready to chastise the rowdy lionesses over their noise, but when he saw Fayola scoop up the grimy-faced cub, he understood what was happening – that there was a reunion – and he instead began preparing to demand an apology from the lionesses on behalf of the hyenas.

As he'd stood in the shadows, listening to Sarabi's questioning of the little one who had made her way back to Pride Rock (the runt could use a lesson in lying; she was appallingly bad at it), he realised that only one of the two missing cubs had returned.

But as the cub stammered through her translucent lies, a plan had begun to take shape in Scar's mind.

If he could bring Nala safely back to Pride Rock, then it would solidify him as a leader worthy of his pride's respect and fealty. It was more than he should have to do – the highest regard should be granted to him simply by virtue of his position – but he guessed nothing came without a small price.

He would have to earn the lionesses' respect, and finding Nala was how he would do it.

"As the leader of this pride, it is only right that *I* go in search of Nala. It is my duty and responsibility to keep the pride safe."

"But—"

"The lionesses have their own duties; they should be attending to those." He looked over at the group of lionesses. "Shouldn't most of you be hunting right now?" He turned back to Sarabi. "Is this how you lead your lionesses? How do you expect them to sustain a search without any sustenance?"

"We wouldn't have to hunt if those hyenas had not raided our kill."

Scar whipped around. "Who said that?"

No one spoke, but irritation radiated from the insolent, disrespectful bunch.

Their discomfort was as satisfying as a loud burp after a good meal. He should not take such pleasure in this, but alas, it would seem being treated as a scoundrel by his own kind had this effect on him. Who would have thought?

"I have made my decision," Scar said. "Zazu and I will fetch Nala."

He turned to Fayola, who still held her cub. What was this one's name again? There were too many of them for him to keep track.

"Now, little one, where did Nala leave you?"

She repeated the story Scar had heard her tell Sarabi before he'd made his presence known.

"If that is the case, I should be able to reach her before she makes it to the Shadowlands," Scar said after she was done.

"But Abena said they took a different route on their way back to Pride Rock," Sarabi said. "Scar, why don't you let Kito and Sefu go one way and you and Zazu can go another. It just makes—"

"No," he said. With the way his luck had played out lately, the two lionesses would find Nala and be back at Pride Rock before he and Zazu reached the north side of the Elephant Graveyard. *He* had to be the one to bring Nala back. No one else.

"Now I will gather Zazu, and we will be on our way."

"Right here, Sire," Zazu said, flying in and landing at Scar's side. "Let's go get that cub. Don't you worry about a thing, Sarabi. We'll get her back. All will be just fine."

Scar blew out an annoyed breath. Maybe he should go alone.

He managed to swallow the words before he could speak them. Besides, Zazu could prove to be useful.

"Let us go," Scar said to the bird.

They took off in the direction of the cut-around that would allow them to bypass the Shadowlands altogether.

"Once we reach the grasslands, I want you to fly ahead to see if you can spot the cub," Scar instructed. "She could not have got much further than the scrubland."

"No problem, Sire. I'm here to be your eyes and ears. We will find Nala. I don't know what that little one was thinking, running off in such a way. Doesn't she know the fright she caused amongst the pride? Sarafina will have to give her a stern talking to when she returns."

"Tone it down," Scar muttered under his breath. If he had to listen to this bird's ceaseless drivel all night, he would not be responsible for what he did next. *Red-billed hornbill stew* had a tasty ring to it.

"Uh, where exactly are we going, Sire?" Zazu asked.

Scar realised the bird had not been around when the cub explained where she and Nala had run off to.

"According to Fayola's littlest—"

"Abena," Zazu provided.

Whatever.

"According to her, Nala wanted a grand adventure in Garamba, but Sarabi believes this has something to do with Simba."

Zazu sighed. "Ah, yes. One of the queen's scouts reported a sighting in Garamba just the other day. But just between you and me, I do not think there is any merit behind it. It seems Queen Sarabi doesn't either; she told the scouts to suspend all searches."

This was the first Scar was hearing of this. He knew Sarabi had dispatched animals throughout the Pride Lands and beyond to look for Simba. She had convinced herself that because his body had not been recovered alongside Mufasa's, it meant he must still be alive. Scar didn't have the heart to tell her how foolishly wrong she was to believe such a thing.

Zazu was still yammering on about poor little Simba.

"Unfortunately, as much as we all hope that Simba survived that stampede, it is time we accept that he is never coming back."

If only they knew that their precious Simba had indeed survived that stampede. But Zazu was right on one front: thanks to Shenzi and her crew, Simba was never coming back. Ever.

Scar let out a chuckle before he could stop himself. He quickly coughed and sniffed in an attempt to cover his gaffe.

"I know, I know," Zazu said. "I still find myself tearing up over the loss too. I guess poor Nala is holding on to one last bit of hope."

"By putting herself at risk? It's foolish," Scar said.

"Well, she *is* just a cub," Zazu said. "And she *did* lose her best friend. Grief can sometimes lead to poor judgement. You know, Sire, one thing I admire about you is how well you handled the loss of both Mufasa and Simba. You were able to step in and take over the reign of Pride Rock despite your obvious grief."

Scar averted his face so the bird couldn't see him roll his eyes.

"Yes, well, I did what I had to do," Scar said. "I knew my pride was depending on me. I could not spend my days wallowing in the sorrow of losing my dear brother and nephew."

"I think Mufasa would be proud of you," Zazu said.

His words rankled.

Why should he care what Mufasa would have thought of him? He did not need approval from a dead king.

Scar was very close to ordering his majordomo to refrain from bringing up his brother to him. Except that he couldn't figure out how to do it without revealing how he really felt about Mufasa. Zazu was irritating, but he was also smart. He would pick up on any animosity Scar revealed.

Instead, he would have to continue playing the role of the bereaved brother and uncle who bravely stepped in to fulfil his duty as king.

"I live to make my brother proud," Scar said.

A brisk wind blew in from the west, bringing with it a faint yet eerily familiar scent.

"Wait," Scar said. He closed his eyes and sniffed the air. It had to be the cub.

"That way," he whispered. In a louder voice, he said, "Zazu, there is a place at the edge of the forest that has a gathering of kopje and other rock formations. I believe she is that way. It would corroborate what that other cub said about the elephant stampede. The elephants making their way to the Masai Mara would have taken that route to avoid the Shadowlands."

Thank goodness he had picked up on that foolish little cub's scent. If Zazu could spot her and direct him where to find her, Scar predicted they would be home before sunrise. He hoped those lionesses had procured more food, because this walk had made him famished. It felt as if he would wilt way before he made it back to Pride Rock.

Yet, what Scar thought would be an easy search turned out to be more difficult than he'd anticipated. Zazu returned to say that he'd found traces of Nala's footsteps but could not find the cub anywhere.

"If she was near the water hole when she brought that other cub back—"

"Abena, Sire. You should really learn the cubs' names."

"That is not my priority at the moment," Scar said between clenched teeth.

"Very true. As you were saying," Zazu said.

"Nala should not have been able to make it very far," Scar said. "Especially in the dark. Wouldn't she be frightened?"

"Oh, I doubt it," Zazu said. "She is braver than her mother gives her credit for. She and Simba would often take off on their own. They gave Sarafina, Sarabi and Mufasa quite a time trying to rein them in."

If this dodo mentioned Mufasa one more time, Scar was going to snatch each of his feathers out one by one.

"Well, her bravery may get her more than just a reprimand," Scar said. It might cost the little fool her life and ruin his chances of winning favour with the lionesses.

Scar was hit with a stunning realisation, something he had not considered when he'd come up with this hasty plan to play the hero. If he did not return with Nala, or if she was harmed in any way before he could get her back to Pride Rock, his pride wouldn't just turn on him – they would likely do *him* harm. They might even kill him.

He had seen it before. Members of a pride swore their allegiance to their pride leader, but if given the grounds to revolt, they would. He'd got the sense that his pride had been seeking a reason to revolt from the moment he took over as leader.

It wasn't just Nala's survival on the line here – it was his own.

"Come, Zazu," Scar said. "Nala is out here alone. We must find her and bring her home safely."

Or it could be deadly for both of them.

CHAPTER EIGHTEEN

The brisk wind blew so hard it cut through Nala's fur, reaching her skin and making her shiver. She didn't know what to make of the strange turn in the weather. It seemed as if the hot and dry days they had experienced for months had suddenly disappeared, replaced by a shift in the weather, starting with the violent storm she and Abena had suffered through. It was chilly, with a heavy dampness that continued to saturate the air.

Nala reminded herself that the chill she couldn't seem to shake from her bones was a small price to pay to get Simba back.

Thank goodness that gazelle had told her how to bypass the Elephant Graveyard. It had saved her time in getting back to the spot where she and Abena had been caught up in that stampede. But just as she attempted to surge ahead in her quest to find Simba, another dilemma reared its head in the form of thick clouds.

They had rolled in just as she'd reached the kopje where she had ridden out the earlier storm, obscuring the moon and stars and slowing her progress. Nala supposed she could try to guess where the bull-shaped cluster of stars was located in the sky, but it was the thought of pressing on with her journey only to discover that she was moving in the wrong direction once the sky cleared that persuaded her to wait for the clouds to move on.

Hopefully, it wouldn't take much longer. She had already lost so much time having to take Abena back to Pride Rock.

She trusted Abena would not reveal where she was heading, but that wasn't her only concern. She also had to think about what she would – or worse, would not – find once she arrived in Garamba. Even if Simba was seen there as the mongoose had reported, it wasn't a guarantee that he would *stay* there. The longer it took her to make it to Garamba, the greater the risk that she would miss out on finding Simba.

She stared up at the sky. Even more clouds had moved in.

At least she knew of a good place to rest. The kopje had been comfortable enough.

Just as she started for the small cluster of boulders, Nala stopped at the sound of rustling in the patch of reedy grasses to her right. She hunched down, unsure if she was about to become the predator or the prey. More rustling. Suddenly a plump hare scrambled out of the grasses.

She grinned. "Predator."

She was still full after eating the hare Abena had hunted for them, but she knew it would not sustain her forever. She would have to hunt before she reached Garamba.

She hadn't thought about how much harder it would be to procure food on her own. There was a reason the lionesses hunted in pairs – and often groups of three or four – and why it took years of practice.

Of course! *That's* what she could do while she waited for the clouds to move. She could practise hunting!

What if she returned to Pride Rock with both Simba *and* a new ability to hunt? What would her pride think of her then?

Excited by the thought, Nala set out in the direction the hare had escaped, her steps measured and methodical. She crouched low to the ground and kept her eyes open for even the slightest movement. The bustling wind made it difficult to distinguish sounds, but the more she concentrated, the better she was able to tell the difference between the rustling leaves and the humming insects.

Her ears perked up at the sound of feet pattering on the rain-softened earth. The *plop, plop, plop* of the mud was unmistakable. Nala held her body as still as a steady baobab trunk, biding her time until the hare revealed its hiding place.

Her patience paid off; she caught a glimpse of the brown-and-white fur out of the corner of her eye. Applying the techniques Abena had shared, Nala slowly backtracked so that she could approach the hare from the rear. Taking cover behind a bush that had just begun sprouting new leaves, she zeroed in on her prey.

Nala pounced…

And caught the hare!

She sat on her hind legs and clenched the hare between her paws before releasing it from her teeth. She stared at the creature in wonderment, hardly able to believe that had just happened.

"I did it," she said in an awed whisper.

It was a small one, but she wouldn't let that take away from her victory. She had never caught a hare before. They were quick, so quick they sometimes proved to be a challenge for grown lionesses who had been hunting for years. Yet, she had caught one by herself! With no other lioness there to help her!

"I did it!" Nala shouted. She held the hare high above her head like the grand prize it was. "I did… it."

Nala looked around and her spirits deflated. What was the use in celebrating her successful hunt if she didn't have the rest of her pridemates to celebrate it with?

She looked at the squirming little hare.

"I caught you," she said excitedly. Her shoulders slumped. "But I guess you wouldn't want to celebrate with me." She tipped her head to the side. "Don't worry, little one. I'm not very hungry. Besides, you need time to get bigger before you're of use to any lion."

She set the hare on the ground and released it from her grip. It dashed into the tall grass.

Nala walked over to the small water hole and lapped the water, her body still tingling from the thrill of having captured the hare.

"Take that, Ola and Kahina," she said.

If only they were around to see it.

But the more she thought about it, the less she wanted to rub her victory in Ola's and Kahina's faces. She wanted them to see that they could rely on her to provide for the pride, as they all would be expected to do one day.

She just wanted to feel like one of them, like she belonged.

Her mother's insistence that she not leave the area near Pride Rock had made her such an outcast, but if Nala was being honest with herself, she could admit that her mother's overprotectiveness was not the only cause for her isolation from the other cubs in the pride. It had started well before Simba left them. Actually, it was *because* of Simba.

Her close relationship with their pride's future king had created a certain amount of distance between herself and the other cubs. It's why Ola and Lindiwe and the others had accused Nala of thinking she was better than the rest of them.

Nala dropped her head to her chest as she accepted an uncomfortable truth about herself.

She *had* thought she was better than the others. Not better, but more important. Not everyone could call themselves the future king's very best friend; how could she not feel special?

She wouldn't allow herself to fall into that way of thinking if she brought Simba back to Pride Rock. *When* she brought him back to Pride Rock. She would make an effort to grow her friendship with *all* the cubs. A close-knit pride was a strong pride, and Nala vowed to make sure her pride remained strong.

She looked up at the sky again, but she knew she would not find any stars. She could barely make out the moon.

The clouds had grown even thicker, and the air had the same kind of weightiness she had felt just before that rainstorm.

It wouldn't rain so soon again, would it?

Three drops pelted her head in quick succession.

"Oh no," Nala said. "Not again."

But yes, here it was. Those three fat drops quickly numbered too many for her to count. The rain bombarded her, pounding the ground in a deluge that seemed to have come from out of nowhere. Nala raced for the kopje, finding the same alcove she had used as shelter earlier.

She rested her chin on her paws and stared out at the torrential downpour. The more she stared, the heavier her eyelids became.

Maybe she should take a short nap. If tonight's storm was anything like the previous one, it would not last long. She could rest for a bit and then she would be even *more* ready to continue on her journey to Garamba.

"That's what I'll do," Nala said around a yawn. "I'll take just a short nap."

She lolled her head to the side and closed her eyes, letting the melodic pounding of the rain carry her to sleep.

CHAPTER NINETEEN

Nala stretched her front legs out ahead of her and twisted around in the small alcove. She thought about opening her eyes but then decided against it. The feel of the sun on her face felt too good. Besides, her mother wasn't here to nag her about waking up.

Wait! The sun?

"Well, are you going to wake up?"

Her mother?

Nala's eyes popped open. She quickly closed them; the bright sun that had felt so good a moment ago now blinded her. Had she slept through the night? She was only supposed to take a short nap to wait out the rain.

Nala groaned.

"That is enough of that, Miss Nala."

She slowly lifted one eye open and frowned, blinking several times. She couldn't be sure if what she was seeing was real or just her mind playing a cruel joke on her.

"Zazu?" Nala croaked.

"You have a lot of explaining to do, missy!"

"What…" She looked around. "What are you doing here?"

"That is my question to *you*. Do you have any idea what you have put your mother and the rest of the pride through? Poor Sarafina has been beside herself with worry," Zazu clucked at her. "Very bad of you, indeed."

Nala closed her eyes and shook her head, hoping that when she opened them, she would find that this was just a bad dream. She opened her eyes. Nope, Zazu was still there.

But how was he here? How had he found her?

She rolled her eyes, feeling like a fool for asking such a ridiculous question when the answer was obvious. This land was far too vast for Zazu to have just happened upon her by chance. No one from their pride had business being around these parts. There was only one logical conclusion: Abena had ratted her out.

Disappointment wedged itself right next to the anger that immediately bubbled up in her. After all that talk about how much they had in common, and how she understood

Nala's plight, Abena had done just what she'd promised she *wouldn't* do.

But had she really expected anything better from a baby cub? Did she think Abena would stare down that wall of angry lionesses and openly defy them? Nala imagined how it all must have played out, with tiny Abena facing an interrogation from the likes of Sarabi, Fayola and Nala's mother. She shivered. She probably would have caved under such pressure too.

No, she couldn't place the blame squarely on Abena. She should have anticipated that this would happen. Maybe if she had, she wouldn't have made the foolish, critical mistake of returning to this exact spot. She should have pushed on for a bit longer, or taken a detour at the start of the gorge. It would have been easy enough to follow the stars from there.

Foolish, foolish, foolish.

"Over here, Sire!" Zazu called.

Sire?

Nala scrambled up on all fours and stared in dismay as Scar climbed up onto the kopje.

Scar? He'd come with Scar?

Nala would have bet anything that her mother would have been the one searching high and low for her, along with the other lionesses. She never would have expected

Scar to have come down from his perch high above Pride Rock to search for her. Their king had left the Pride Lands? For her? It seemed unreal.

"Nala," Scar said with a relieved breath. "Thank heavens you are safe. You have given everyone such a fright."

"That is what I told her, Sire. This was very, very bad of you, Nala. You know the pride is still hurting after the loss of Mu—"

Scar cut him off. "Zazu, leave me with the cub. I would like to have a word with her."

"Yes, yes," Zazu said. "She deserves a stern talking to. Although, Sire, I'm sure Sarafina would rather we bring her back to Pride Rock as soon as possible. Maybe you can wait—"

"Zazu," Scar said in a voice that brooked no argument.

"Of course, Sire," Zazu said.

Nala watched as he flitted away. She looked off into the distance, towards the Shadowlands. She sure could use a nice, disruptive elephant stampede right about now.

"Nala."

She finally returned her attention to Scar. Censure coated his expression.

It would have been bad enough to have her mother reprimand her for running away, or even Sarabi. But to have the leader of their pride be the one to find her? How embarrassing!

At least Scar appeared to be alone, which meant she would be spared having to face this humiliation in front of the entire pride. Ola and the others would have teased her relentlessly if they were to witness this. They probably still would.

"Nala, Nala, Nala," Scar began. "What were you thinking, going off on some grand adventure at your age? And taking Abena with you?"

"She asked to come along," Nala said. "I tried to get her to stay at Pride Rock, but she wouldn't listen."

Scar looked down his long nose at her. "It would appear that Abena isn't the only cub who has trouble listening to her elders. You have caused your mother much worry," he said.

Nala swallowed and looked down at her paws. "I know."

"You should be ashamed of yourself, Nala. This little stunt was not funny. It was reckless. You must never do such a thing again."

"I won't," Nala said.

She wasn't sure which was worse, having to sit there and listen to Scar's lecture, or thinking about the one she knew she would get from her mother when she returned home. Would it stop at those two, or would she be subjected to reprimands from the other lionesses as well?

She grimaced at the thought of sitting in the middle of the clearing while Sarabi, Kito and all the others took turns scolding her. She could just imagine the cubs peeking down from the landing on Pride Rock, snickering while Nala suffered through her punishment.

She still wasn't sure why Scar was the one who had been tasked with searching for her. It had been her hope that Sarabi would buy the story she and Abena had come up with – that Nala was safe and would return to Pride Rock soon. She had assumed if Sarabi *did* choose to send out a search party, it would consist of fellow lionesses. Hunters like Sefu and Kito, who were some of the best in their pride at tracking down prey.

Nala grimaced. In a way, she *had* turned herself into prey, hadn't she?

Still, Scar's presence confused her. He didn't do anything around camp. She regularly heard the lionesses whispering while at the water hole that Scar was a poor substitute for Mufasa. She even heard Thandi say that Simba would have been more effective as a leader, even with him still being a young cub. Yet, Scar was the one they had sent?

Did this mean the others had not wanted to search for her? Were they so angry that she had sneaked away, and had put Abena in danger by doing so, that they hadn't even cared to come looking?

A painful tightness constricted Nala's throat.

She'd heard stories of prides abandoning their young and had wondered what a cub could possibly do to make their entire pride turn their back on them. Was it something like this? Had her running away been the last straw?

While Scar continued to drone on about why she should be ashamed of the worry she had caused everyone, Nala tried to figure out what her next steps should be. This was only a setback; it was not the end of her hunt for Simba. She couldn't give up. Not now. Not when it was possibly the only thing that would earn her forgiveness from the rest of her pride.

And not when she had proved that she could do this!

She'd hunted down a hare. A small one, but that didn't matter. And look how quickly she had navigated her way back to this spot. If those clouds and the rain had not appeared last night, who knows how far she would be right now. She could possibly have made it to Garamba.

One thing Nala *did* know was that she could not return to Pride Rock with Scar.

She had been lucky to slip away the first time. She would have zero chance of escaping again. Her mother would keep watch over her like one of those massive birds that circled high above the water hole, only to dive into the water and come up with a fish between their teeth.

She knew she was risking the same fate were she to get to Garamba and discover that Simba wasn't there and then return without him, but at least she would have tried. To go back now would mean she'd done all this for nothing.

No, not for nothing. If she had never left Pride Rock, she wouldn't have got that hunting lesson from Abena and she never would have had the opportunity to prove to herself that she could catch that hare.

But it wasn't enough. She wanted more. She wanted – *needed* – to find her best friend.

"Have I made myself clear, Nala?"

She looked up at Scar and blinked several times. "Umm... yes?" Nala answered. She had no idea what he'd said, but Scar didn't seem to care.

"Very well. We shall be on our way." He hitched the brow with the huge gash above it and grinned. "Sarafina is going to be thrilled to have you back. All the lionesses will be. Who knows, maybe they will be so inspired by your return that they'll hunt us down a couple of okapis. We can have a feast to celebrate."

"That sounds delightful, Sire," Zazu said as he swooped in. "This is, indeed, a cause for celebration. However, I doubt you will be allowed to celebrate much, Miss Nala. I know for certain that your mother will give you a serious talking to."

Nala rolled her eyes. As if she needed Zazu to tell her that.

"Let us get going," Scar said. "I need a nap." He looked down at Nala and, in a stern voice, said, "You stick close to me, do you hear me?"

"Yes," Nala lied.

They began the trek back to Pride Rock, with Scar leading the way and Zazu flying just above his right shoulder. Nala walked several paces behind him, waiting for the best moment to make her move.

They arrived at the edge of the forest, where the area thick with trees began to thin into the scrubland that would lead them into their Pride Lands. Nala sucked in a deep breath, turned and ran.

She cut through the trees. Had Scar noticed she wasn't behind him yet? She was too afraid to look back. It would slow her down. Instead, she surged forwards, sprinting over downed tree trunks and moss-covered rocks.

Until, suddenly, her feet were no longer on the ground.

Nala let out a loud squeal as she was scooped up into bony arms. The next thing she knew, she was dangling by her back leg. She looked up into the face of the monkey who had captured her.

Then they took off, swinging from one tree to the next.

CHAPTER TWENTY

Hartebeest or eland?

Scar couldn't decide what he was in the mood for tonight. He wanted something he had not eaten in a while. Something good.

Oh, maybe an Ankole cow!

Yes, that was it. He would demand the lionesses bring him a nice and meaty Ankole cow. He wanted two: one just for him and one for Shenzi and her crew to share. The hyenas deserved it for the undue blame that had been cast upon them by the pride. Sarabi and her lot of judgemental lionesses had been so sure that the hyenas were behind Nala's disappearance, when it was the cub who had run away on her own. He would order that insolent one, Thandi, to present the offering to the hyenas. Wouldn't that be delightful?

Scar realised he was having too much fun coming up with ways to make the lionesses thank him for bringing Nala home safely, but was there really such a thing as too much fun? Besides, he was only commanding they grant him what he was already due.

"All those back at Pride Rock will be so very happy to welcome Miss Nala home, and they have *you* to thank for it," Zazu said. "Well, you and me. *I* am the one who actually found her, but it was *you* who convinced her to come back."

The bird had not taken a moment to catch his breath, but because he was mostly praising Scar this time, Scar let him continue.

"And I think holding a grand feast is a remarkable idea," Zazu said. "It has been such a long time since we have had reason to celebrate. Not since – did you hear that, Sire?" Zazu asked. "It sounded like a shriek."

Scar was about to ask Zazu what he was yammering on about this time but decided it wasn't worth the effort it would take to pretend he cared.

"There it goes again," Zazu said. "Miss Nala, did you— Miss Nala! Where did she go?"

Scar stopped and whipped around. Nala was no longer following them.

He growled. Why hadn't he ordered the little troublemaker to walk in front of him? He should have expected she would pull something like this.

Scar started to retrace their steps, but then he thought better of it. Why should he expend the effort to go running after Nala? So the lionesses back at Pride Rock could groom her to be as defiant and disrespectful of him as they all were? If the little scamp wanted to go on her adventure so badly, who was he to deny her? She could run all the way to Morocco for all he cared.

"Sire, what are you doing? Are you not going to go after Nala?" Zazu asked in a frantic voice.

"No," Scar answered.

"No? But... but..." the bird sputtered, flapping his wings as if he were trying to put out a fire. "But you promised Sarabi you would find her."

"I *did* find her, did I not? I fulfilled my promise."

"But... it does not count if you do not bring her back to Pride Rock."

"Sure it does," Scar said. "If I say it counts, it counts. I'm the king. I make the rules."

Zazu zigzagged through the air, going back and forth as he ranted about the dangers Nala faced and how it was Scar's duty to retrieve her.

"Maybe Nala should have thought about that before

running off a second time," Scar said. "No, make that a third time. She could have returned when Abena did but chose not to. Sometimes in life, one must learn their lesson the hard way."

He had been reluctant to return without Nala in tow, but even the lionesses would have to give him credit for doing what he said he would do. Nala had made her choice. He would wash his paws of this entire matter.

"She is just a cub! She does not know any better," Zazu said. "Sire, we cannot leave her out here!"

It seemed his majordomo was forgetting his place. He was not the one who called the shots here – that was Scar's job, and his alone.

"I have made my decision," Scar said. Then, with a shrug, he added, "If you want to bring her back to her mother so badly, you go after her. As for me? I'm going home to take a nap."

"These are not the actions befitting a king!" Zazu squawked and took off.

Scar started to call him on his insolence, but what could he say? Zazu was right.

You're no Mufasa.

He batted away the voice in his head. He did not care to be like his brother in any way. Scar knew without a doubt what Mufasa would have done in this situation. He had witnessed it first-paw, the way he'd charged into that gorge when he learnt Simba was there. He hadn't given a thought to his own life. It didn't matter that Nala was not his cub; Mufasa would have done the same for her. For any of the cubs in their pride.

Scar hunched his shoulders. He guessed he still had some growing to do. He just didn't have that instinct, to put another's life above his own.

"Sire! Sire!" Zazu zipped past him and then quickly turned to hover in front of Scar's face. "You must come quickly!"

Scar rolled his eyes. "Back so soon?"

"Macaques," Zazu screeched. "A whole pack of them. They've cub-napped, Nala!"

Scar was actually surprised by the hint of alarm that emerged within him. The macaques around these parts were known for their aggressiveness. The cub was truly in grave danger if a pack of them had snatched her.

"Sire, please! Think of Sarafina. It will devastate her if those primates hurt Nala. They could kill her, Sire!"

Scar couldn't help thinking of how losing Simba had broken Sarabi. Sarafina wasn't nearly as strong as his sister-in-law. The lioness would, in all likelihood, go mad if a pack of violent macaques were to tear her cub apart limb by limb.

Wait a minute…

How much more would the pride revere him if he returned to Pride Rock with Nala safe and sound, but with the added story of saving her from a pack of murdering macaques? He could count on Zazu to regale them all with the harrowing tale; his majordomo did have quite a flair for the dramatic.

The lionesses would have no choice but to reward his bravery with the one thing he sought from them: unconditional respect and allegiance.

"Where have the macaques taken her, Zazu?" Scar asked. "Point me in the direction."

"This way!" Zazu shouted.

They took off towards the thicket of wild bushland that initiated the gradual transition from tame savanna to unruly jungle.

"I knew you would do the right thing, Sire. I never doubted you for a moment."

Scar ignored the bird as he trudged across a turbid creek bed, the recent rains creating a thick sludge at the bottom of it. He would have to submerge himself in the nearest water hole as soon as he rescued that little troublemaker.

Nala was smart to have come this way; Scar had to give her that. Looking at the denseness of the bushland up ahead, there were countless places to hide. Of course, that now worked against her. Scar assumed she hadn't anticipated getting snatched by a band of savage macaques when she'd made her sneaky escape.

Life lessons. They were all around.

"Zazu, go ahead. See if you can spot where they've taken her," Scar called.

He did not have fighting off macaques as part of today's agenda. However, if this is what it took to show Sarabi and the others that he should be the one to lead them, so be it. Good ol' Scar to the rescue.

He approached the entrance to the bushland and immediately encountered sticker bushes. Scar yelped as the painful burrs clamped onto his paws and legs.

He would demand those lionesses feed him Ankole cattle for the next month as repayment for having to go through this. Stopping to remove burrs was out of the question, so Scar did his best to ignore the ache in his paws. The sooner he got to Nala, the sooner they could leave this dense forest and all its deadly trappings.

She had better hope he got to her before those macaques decided to tear her apart.

As he travelled through the labyrinth of jackalberry, marula and bush willows, something Scar had not considered began to run through his mind. Would the lionesses grow suspicious if he returned to Pride Rock as the sole witness to yet another of his pride's cubs meeting an untimely demise? It wasn't even of his doing this time, unlike Simba's little accident.

But that wouldn't matter to them. All they would see was a second cub gone, with him as the one who had to break the bad news. So many of the lionesses already did not trust him. If Nala perished at the hands of those macaques, his pride may start to question his involvement.

He had to get her back. If he didn't, he would never get those lionesses to accept him as their leader, especially after he had ordered them to remain at Pride Rock so that he could prove his worth as their king by retrieving Nala on his own.

Scar's chest tightened with his anxious, accelerated breaths.

"I'll save you, Nala," he whispered. "But only because those lionesses will have my hide if I don't."

CHAPTER TWENTY-ONE

Intense, violent throbbing pulsated from the spots where Nala's head banged against the thick tree limbs. She tried to shield it as best she could, but with the way she dangled from the monkey's tight grip, it was difficult for her to control her own body.

Her stomach roiled with the up-and-down motion as they swung from tree to tree. Not to mention the heart-stopping fear that the monkey would lose his tight grip and she would go plummeting to the ground. Her mind was a jumbled mess – with her wanting him to free her yet afraid that he would do just that.

Their ear-piercing screeches were the worst sound she had ever heard, even worse than the cackle of the hyenas.

It made screaming for help impossible – not that she would even try at this point. She was certain the monkeys had taken her too far into the jungle for Scar or Zazu to hear her. She would rather conserve what little energy she had left, though she wasn't sure why.

She had no idea where they were headed, she just knew with a gut-wrenching certainty that she would never see her home again.

Nala began sobbing, whether for herself or her mother, she wasn't sure. She imagined the heartache her mother would feel when Scar and Zazu returned without her. She had considered the possibility of getting injured or worse before she'd left Pride Rock, but Nala had thought it would surely be worth it when she brought Simba back to reign as king.

But getting captured by these monkeys changed everything. There would be no return to Pride Rock with Simba. And now it seemed she would not be returning either. Nala doubted she would survive the rest of the day in the company of these monkeys.

Of all the ways she could have met her death, this was quite a letdown. She would have preferred battling a leopard or a white rhinoceros. To be killed by a pack of monkeys was pathetic.

Her head bounced on another thick branch, and for a

moment, she only saw black. She started to screech, then realised it was because she had closed her eyes. Pathetic.

The monkey swung to another tree, and Nala shut her eyes again as a bunch of leaves slapped her in the face.

After what seemed like a lifetime, their journey through the dense forest came to an abrupt stop. She grew even dizzier as she continued to hang upside down from where the monkey held her by her back right leg. From what she could make out, they were in an acacia tree. Its feather-like leaves shaded them from the sun, while the tangle of smooth underbranches created the perfect resting spot for the dozens of squalling monkeys.

The noise was relentless. Part of her wanted them to just do whatever they were planning to do to her so that she would be freed from this awful racket.

The monkey that held her started to jump up and down on the branch, and Nala immediately took back her previous thought. She wasn't ready to die.

She wanted her mummy more than she ever had before.

Before Nala knew what was happening, another monkey swung to the branch where she was being held and grabbed her left foreleg. He jerked her towards him, but the monkey that had captured her wouldn't let go of her back leg. It jerked even harder.

Oh no. No, please.

It went on like this for several minutes, a literal tug-of-war with her as the rope. They were going to rip her to pieces. Nala heard an awful cracking sound a second before the blinding pain registered in her front leg. Was it broken?

Did it matter? Her entire body would soon be splintered and tossed about this forest like the bones of a freshly eaten gazelle.

Just when Nala was certain that the life-ending tug was about to happen, she heard the welcome sound of a fierce lion roar. The monkeys stopped their screaming and jumping, all becoming instantly, perfectly still. She wouldn't have believed it if she had not just witnessed it with her own eyes.

The lion roared again. Then she heard, "Nala! Where are you?"

Scar! That roar belonged to Scar!

"Up here! Scar, I'm up here!" Nala yelled.

Her shouts sent the monkeys into a frenzy. Nala was afraid they would take off before Scar could reach her, but a moment later she heard his wondrous roar again. She looked down to see him climbing the tree and had never felt more relieved than when she felt Scar clamp down on her scruff. He batted away the monkey that had held her captive.

Chaos ensued.

Scar dashed down the acacia tree. Instead of retreating, as Nala assumed the monkeys would do, they followed. At least a dozen of them converged on her and Scar.

He set her on the ground and motioned for her to get behind him.

Nala's heart slammed against her chest in the same way her head had slammed against those branches. She looked on in horror as Scar crouched low. His deep, rumbling growl was so menacing even *she* was scared, despite knowing that he was on her side.

The monkeys encircled them. The biggest of the crew, the one that had snatched her, lifted his arms in a show of aggression. The others followed, howling and flapping their arms.

Nala held her breath.

She had never heard of a pack of monkeys defeating a lion, but there was a first time for everything.

The head monkey charged at Scar. Nala looked on in astonishment as Scar leapt forwards, catching the monkey mid-air in his mouth. He clamped his teeth on its right leg, then pulled the monkey from his mouth with both paws. Scar slammed the monkey on the ground so hard it made Nala wince.

That was all it took. The others gathered their wounded friend and took off, shrieking their displeasure.

Nala stared in disbelief at the spot where Scar had thrown the monkey. She was bloodied and bruised, and her leg felt as if it would fall off, but she was alive! She had been certain that she would not live to see another day, yet here she was. Alive!

Thanks to Scar.

He turned, and for a moment, Nala thought that maybe she wouldn't live to see another day after all. His expression was murderous, that ugly scar that slashed across his eyebrow puckered.

"What were you thinking, you little fool?" he snapped. "Do you know what those macaques could have done to you?"

Nala bobbed her head in a frantic nod.

She had spent the past half hour picturing all the awful ways those monkeys could have killed her. They could have ripped her body apart or stomped on her head until she ceased to exist. But they didn't get the chance to do any of that because of Scar.

All of a sudden, she was overcome by a rush of emotions: relief, gratitude, anguish. They overwhelmed her, robbing the breath from her lungs.

Before she could comprehend what she was doing, Nala rushed over to Scar and collapsed against his chest.

"Thank you, thank you, thank you."

She knew this wasn't the response Scar had expected to his question. She should apologise for putting herself in a position that forced him to have to rescue her, but she couldn't help it. She was so grateful to be alive. All she could think about was how close she had come to being a collection of cub limbs sprinkled around the forest.

"Thank you, thank you, thank you," she repeated over and over again.

Scar stiffened. A moment later, she felt him lightly patting her back with his big paw as if he thought he would hurt her. Or maybe as if he didn't necessarily want to touch her. She couldn't blame him; she was sure she looked a fright.

"Oh, Miss Nala!" Zazu flew up to them. He was in full-on hysterics. "Are you injured? Should I find raw wood plants? How do we dress a wound, Sire? We should dress her wounds, and check for broken bones! And, oh my, what about a head injury! I did not consider a head injury! Oh, Nala, why do you insist on putting me through this agony!"

"ZAZU!" Scar bellowed so loud he sent his majordomo sailing back into the trunk of the acacia tree. "Pull yourself together!"

"But look at her, Sire! She is at death's door!"

Scar peered down at her, and Nala had to fight not to squirm.

"You have taken a beating, haven't you?" he said.

She nodded. The motion caused her to sway.

"Oh, for heaven's sake," Scar said, scooping her up just before she hit the ground. "So now I have to literally carry you back to Pride Rock. Lucky me."

"No," Nala said. Then she moaned.

"Well, you certainly cannot walk," Zazu said. "Not in the state you're in."

"I can't go back," she said. "Not yet."

If only she could rest for a few minutes, she would be fine. The wooziness would subside, and she could think more clearly.

"Let us be gone from this jungle," Zazu said. "If we leave now, we can make it back to Pride Rock before the sun sets."

The sunset. The stars. She needed the stars.

"No!" Nala said, suddenly alert. She could not return to Pride Rock yet again. She had to keep moving forwards.

"Nala, this little adventure of yours is over," Scar said.

"It… it can't be," Nala said "Not yet. I have to make it to… to somewhere important."

A weight settled in the pit of her stomach.

Should she tell Scar where she was heading? She'd vowed to keep the reason for her trek to Garamba a secret from everyone, and especially from the adult members of their pride, but Nala did not see any other way out of this. If she didn't tell Scar, he would cart her back to Pride Rock. He might still demand that they return even if she did tell him, but she had to take that chance. She could not risk returning home.

But could she trust Scar?

She knew the lionesses did not, for reasons she didn't fully understand. Even though they deferred to him as their pride's leader, there had been numerous times over the last six months when Nala had sensed tension when Scar's name was mentioned. And she had a feeling that it was about more than just his insistence that their pride accept the hyenas as part of their family. Their distrust went deeper.

However, Scar had never given *her* a reason not to trust him. And he had just saved her from certain death.

She had to take this chance.

"I am not on an adventure," Nala said. "Well, I guess I am, but an adventure is not the reason I left Pride Rock. I am on an important mission."

Scar released an exasperated sigh and rolled his eyes. "I know all about your plans to go to Garamba, Nala."

Her breath caught in her throat.

Had Abena shared everything about their time together?

"You overheard the mongoose telling Sarabi that Simba was seen there, but you are on a fool's mission,"

Scar continued. "How many places have there been Simba sightings since the wildebeest stampede? He was seen near Lake Malawi, and then in Dodoma. Where will he show up next? Zanzibar?"

"But this is different," Nala said.

"Of course it is." He rolled his eyes. "Tell me, what makes Garamba any different from all the others?"

Nala bit the inside of her cheek, uncertainty about trusting Scar warring with the awareness of what she knew she must do. This had always been her and Simba's secret, but it could no longer be. Not if she wanted to save him.

"Because Simba and I talked about going there," Nala said. "We always said that if we ever left Pride Rock, we would go straight to Garamba."

She thought she saw a flash of interest in his expression, but then he shook his head and said, "Who doesn't dream of going to Garamba? It's wonderful there. I've been there a time or two myself. It means nothing."

"But Rafiki saw him there too."

"Rafiki?" Scar asked. She had definitely caught his interest this time.

Nala nodded excitedly. "The mongoose reported that Rafiki had a vision of Simba in a cave. I believe it is the Blue Grotto in Garamba; that's the one place we talked of visiting the most."

"I don't know about this," Zazu said. "That still seems like a bit of a stretch to me, Miss Nala."

Nala seared him with a scathing stare. She did not need Zazu chiming in with his doubts. She was close to convincing Scar; she could feel it.

"Think about it, Scar," Nala said. "Simba's body was never found. I believe he survived that stampede in the gorge that day, and for some reason, he chose to leave Pride Rock and go to Garamba. Simba is alive," she said. "I have to bring him home."

She set her paw on Scar's much larger one.

"Please," Nala begged. "Help me bring Simba home."

CHAPTER TWENTY-TWO

Scar did his best to keep his expression neutral, but inside he was roiling. He could not possibly have heard Nala correctly. It was incomprehensible.

"You say that you and Simba spoke of going to Garamba?" Scar asked her.

She nodded, her eyes sparkling with a mixture of excitement and apprehension. "We talked about it all the time. We would listen to the animals around the water hole that had just returned from there, and they always made it seem so magical, especially the Blue Grotto. It sounded so different from Pride Rock. We wanted to see what made it so special. We promised each other that we would go there one day."

"But it does not make sense, Miss Nala," Zazu said. "If Simba survived that stampede, why would he not return to Pride Rock? I do not care how much he wanted to see this grotto, he would have known that everyone would be worried about him, especially Queen Sarabi."

Scar gritted his teeth. He had warned Zazu about referring to Sarabi as their queen

"I don't know why," Nala said. "There must be a reason he didn't return; something important."

Yes, something like his uncle telling Simba that his pride would blame him for their king's death if he ever showed his face at Pride Rock again.

Scar found himself in an unfamiliar state, feeling both worried and confused. He didn't like it. He much preferred being in control of what was happening around him. But Nala's revelations made him feel the opposite of in control.

Could he trust what the cub was saying?

And what was this about Rafiki? Scar had not heard a word from that one since his brother's death. Mufasa's trusted adviser had not even pretended that he would stick around and serve Scar once he took over as leader of the pride.

But Scar could not deny that there was something remarkably uncanny about the mandrill's visions. Rafiki had predicted Simba's birth before Sarabi even knew she was carrying Mufasa's heir in her womb. The warnings he had given the pride over the years had saved them from enemy invasions, devastating storms and more. If something about Simba had recently appeared to Rafiki, Scar could not dismiss it out of paw. He may not like the mandrill, but he respected his abilities.

But Rafiki *had* to be wrong this time. Simba could not be alive. Yes, the cub had somehow managed to escape the hooves of those wildebeests, but Scar had set his hyenas on him with specific instructions to kill the brat. Shenzi had assured him that Simba was dead.

Unless…

Scar stood up straight. Something prickled at the back of his neck. It was the same feeling he got whenever Simba was mentioned around the hyenas. They would get nervous, and Shenzi would always find a way to change the subject.

Scar saw red. Blood red.

Heat pulsed through his body as his heart began to pound within his chest. Those mangy fools had lied to him about taking care of Simba all those months ago. That was the only explanation.

"Uh, Sire, are you okay?" Zazu asked. "You are looking somewhat unwell."

Scar sucked in a deep breath. He needed to calm down; it was the only way he would be able to think clearly.

"I am just trying to make sense of all this," Scar said

as he began to pace back and forth along the spongy jungle floor. "This is a lot to take in."

Or maybe it wasn't.

He could not be too hasty here. There was a high probability that Nala was mistaken. She was nothing but a cub, one who missed her best friend. She wanted all these puzzle pieces to fit together because she wanted to believe that Simba was still alive. But that didn't mean it was true.

As for Rafiki. Well, who knew if that old monkey even had all his marbles, or if the mongoose who delivered news of Rafiki's vision was accurate in his reporting?

If his nephew *was* still alive, there was no way he would have stayed away from his mother all these months. Simba would have made his way back to Pride Rock, one way or another.

Scar recalled the words he'd spoken to him outside the gorge.

Run away, Simba. Run. Run away, and never return.

Would Simba have truly taken that warning to heart if he had survived? It was possible, but unlikely. And if he did, he would not stay away forever.

"Nala, I am sure you want to believe that Simba is still alive," Scar said. "But do you really think he would have made it to Garamba on his own?"

"*I* made it partway there on *my* own," she pointed out.

Scar was amused by her pluckiness. Should he remind her that those macaques had nearly ripped her apart?

Remembering how close Nala had come to meeting her demise made Scar even more doubtful that Simba would have reached that jungle on his own. He was getting himself worked up over nothing.

"Well, Nala, perhaps my nephew was not as brave as you are," Scar told her. "He was still a young cub when that stampede happened."

She shook her head. "No. You're wrong. Simba is the bravest cub I know. I know he made it to Garamba."

"But, Miss Nala, if you suspected Simba was in Garamba, why did you not share this news with Queen Sarabi?" Zazu asked. "She deserves to know."

"Because if I told her, she would have stopped me from going to search for Simba myself. *I* want to be the one who finds him," she said.

"You want to be the hero," Scar surmised. Of course she did. Didn't everyone?

"No, that's not it," Nala said. "I want to find him so that I can make up for letting him go to the gorge on his own that day." Her voice broke as she choked out the words.

She sniffed and dropped her head, then in a small voice, Nala continued, "Simba asked me to join him the day he went to the gorge, but we had just got in trouble for sneaking away to the Elephant Graveyard, and I was afraid we would get caught again. Or that Zazu would rat us out," she said, shooting the bird a mean look.

"I was only doing my job," Zazu protested.

Nala didn't address Zazu. Instead, she continued, "I just keep thinking that maybe if I had gone with Simba like he'd asked me to, I could have talked him out of going down to the gorge, and then King Mufasa wouldn't have had to rescue him. And they would both still be here."

She hiccuped on the last word, her head hanging so low it nearly touched the ground.

"Oh, Miss Nala," Zazu said. "Have you been blaming yourself for what happened this entire time?"

She had. It was more than obvious to Scar. Poor little fool. Taking the blame for something *he* had done.

Scar suddenly realised that his heart was not made completely of stone. He actually felt sorry for Nala. Well, he almost felt sorry for her.

Nala's misplaced blame was not his concern at the moment. *His* concern was his nephew and the possibility that he was not, in fact, dead. The nephew that, if he *was* alive, would threaten Scar's place as ruler of their pride.

Scar was stymied by a perplexing bout of indecisiveness.

Could he trust the word of a guilt-ridden cub who had just spent the last ten minutes dangling from the arm of a wild macaque? Could he afford not to?

He immediately knew the answer to that question. He could not leave anything to chance, especially something as important as Simba possibly returning to Pride Rock.

Just the thought of what would happen if Mufasa's spawn ever came near their home again sent a shiver down Scar's spine. He would tell the pride everything about that day at the gorge. Scar knew his sister-in-law well enough to know that it would not take much for Sarabi to put the pieces of the puzzle together. She just had to think about who had the most to gain if both Mufasa and Simba were no longer here.

"Are you sure about this, Nala?" Scar asked.

She nodded. "Yes. Simba is in Garamba. I can *feel* it."

"And if he is not?" Scar asked.

She dropped her head again and pushed at a pebble with her grimy paw. "If he is not there, that means he isn't anywhere. But I have to be sure," she quickly added. "That is why I must continue my journey. If I don't, then I will always wonder."

So would he.

Scar knew he wouldn't rest easy until he went to Garamba and saw for himself that Simba was not there *and* that he had never been there.

"Okay," Scar said.

Nala's head shot up. She looked at him, her little eyes filled with hope. "Okay?"

"Okay?!" Zazu screeched. "Sire, you cannot be serious."

He was deadly serious.

If he only had Nala's word to go on, Scar probably wouldn't bother, but he could not discount Rafiki's vision. It changed everything. If there was even the slightest possibility that Simba was still alive, he must find him.

And eliminate him.

"Of course I am serious," Scar said to his majordomo. "You heard what Nala said: Simba has always had plans to go to Garamba."

"But, Sire, you cannot think—"

"Silence, Zazu," Scar warned. "If you do not think it is worth searching for Simba, you can go back home."

"How could you say such a thing," Zazu sputtered, flapping his wings indignantly. "There is nothing I want more than to find young Simba alive and well."

And that, Scar realised, was exactly why Scar would have to kill him, along with Simba and Nala.

The way he saw it, there was only one solution to securing his position as the one true king of Pride Rock. He would have to make certain there was no possible way Mufasa's heir could ever usurp what Scar had already claimed as his own, and guarantee that any witnesses would not bring word back to his pride of what he had done.

He should have taken care of this himself from the very beginning, instead of entrusting such an important job to those hyenas. He would have to rethink their place in his kingdom when he returned home as well.

But he would worry about the hyenas later. Right now, his sole focus was to uncover if there was any truth to Nala's assertions.

Scar assessed her. She was pretty banged up, but at least she no longer appeared to be near fainting. He wondered if he should just get rid of both Nala and Zazu now.

No, no. Nala would be the perfect distraction for Simba. His nephew would be so preoccupied with his best friend that he wouldn't see Scar's attack. Once he found and eliminated Simba, Scar knew he would have to come up with a plausible story that would explain how all in their party had perished but for him. It would be a hard sell, but he would figure out a way to do it. He must.

He lowered his head so that he could look Nala in the eyes.

"This will be a treacherous journey to find Simba. Are you sure about this, Nala?"

"Yes," she said.

"Then it is settled," Scar said. "We are continuing on to Garamba."

"And I shall go back to Pride Rock to inform Sarabi of these new developments," Zazu said.

"You shall do no such thing," Scar said. He reached up and snatched the bird before he could fly off. He would take pleasure in finally ridding himself of his majordomo.

"But, Sire, why not?" Zazu asked.

"Because Sarabi does not need to know."

"But he is her son. Surely—"

"I don't care what he is!" he snapped.

Scar caught Nala's reaction out of the corner of his eye. She jerked back and her eyes narrowed with a hint of distrust.

He quickly regained his composure. He could not allow Nala to suspect that he had anything but Simba's best interest at heart.

"Think of what it would do to Sarabi if it turns out the mongoose provided faulty information," he said, his demeanour more composed. "Do you really want to put her through such agony a second time?"

"Oh, no. I would never want to cause Queen Sarabi more pain."

"I didn't think so," Scar said. "You will continue on with us. I need you to fly ahead and assess the path for any dangers."

Scar looked back at Nala. "There are a multitude of

ways to reach Garamba. Why did you decide to take this particular route?"

"Because Simba and I were told to follow the bull-shaped stars," she answered.

Ah, she was following Taurus. She was certainly a smart one, wasn't she? He would have to remember that as they made their way through this land.

Fortunately, he did not have to rely on the stars to guide him to Garamba. A quick jaunt through the Otze Forest and around Mount Kei should get them there by nightfall.

"I know an even shorter route. Come, Nala. Let us go find my dear nephew."

CHAPTER TWENTY-THREE

Sarabi stood within the shadow of the ancient baobab tree, away from the rest of the lionesses and other animals that grazed or availed themselves of a cool drink at the water hole. She liked to come here from time to time. There was something comforting about observing the day-to-day life of the pride from this vantage point.

Unfortunately, the tranquil scene did little to bring her comfort today. Sarabi feared that if Scar was unsuccessful in retrieving Nala, her pride would never know peace or comfort again.

They had all tried to keep up a brave front in the face of the tragedy playing out within their pride in real time. There had been a steady stream of lionesses coming to her all day, seeking guidance about what they should do, hinting at defying Scar's edict and putting together a search for Nala.

With every hour that passed without word from Scar, Sarabi was tempted to do that very thing. But she was keenly aware of the consequences that could result from defying the leader of their pride. If she were to go against Scar's orders, it would lead to chaos.

She had heard of such things happening before. The next time Scar issued a directive the lionesses disagreed with, they would push for Sarabi to defy it again. Or, worse, they would start to openly rebel against Scar on their own, without waiting to get her guidance on the matter.

What was to stop them from refusing to obey her commands when they disagreed with her?

Sarabi could not risk it. There *must* be order and a hierarchy for a pride to remain successful. One crack in the chain of command and the entire pride would crumble.

She would wait this out for as long as she could, though she knew it would not be easy. Putting her trust in her brother-in-law at a time like this was, by far, one of the most difficult things Sarabi could imagine doing. Scar was not a leader, no matter what the line of succession had decreed. It took more than just the blood running through one's veins to be a leader.

Please, let him be better at tracking down cubs than he is at running this pride.

Sarabi made her way to the water hole but kept to the western edge of it, some distance away from where several of the lionesses had clustered together with their cubs. She could not handle their questioning her right now.

But it would seem she would not be granted the peace she so desperately sought. The moment she lowered her head to lap at the water, Sarabi noticed Kito walking with purpose, her eyes set on her.

She loved her sister, but she did not want to speak to her right now.

Kito did not bother with a greeting. She simply said, "They should be back by now."

Sarabi could not argue with her. She had thought the same. If what Abena had told them was true, then Nala should not have got very far after bringing the younger cub back to Pride Rock. It should not be taking Scar this long to retrieve her. Unless he had got turned around, or if Nala had taken a different route.

Sarabi told this to Kito, but it didn't satisfy her sister.

"It is yet another reason why we should spread out in teams to look for her," Kito argued. "Nala is smart. I'm sure she considered that we would set out to search for her. It only makes sense that she wouldn't take the same route.

It increases her chances of not being found."

Sarabi shut her eyes tight. Kito was not saying anything she had not already thought herself. A constant stream of various scenarios continued to run through her mind. Things that could have happened to Nala already. Things that could be happening to her at this very moment. None of it was good.

"I just do not understand: why would Scar insist on going after Nala alone when we all could be out looking for her?" Kito asked. "We are all better hunters than he is."

"It is not our job to question our ki— our leader's actions," Sarabi said.

"Maybe it is time someone *starts* questioning him," Kito said. "Because something is not right about this."

"We cannot," Sarabi said. "The last thing this pride needs right now is an insurrection." She lowered her voice. "We may not like it, but Scar is the leader of our pride. If it is his wish to retrieve Nala on his own, without the help of anyone but his majordomo, then that is how it must be."

She could tell Kito wanted to argue further but held back out of respect for Sarabi's position within their pride. It was precisely why Sarabi refused to question or openly defy Scar. She had to set an example; being insubordinate would encourage the other lionesses to behave the same way, which would lead to chaos. It was her job to remain calm. Her level-headedness was the only thing keeping this pride together.

Yet, as a leader, Sarabi could also tell that things could not go on this way. The lionesses were becoming too agitated waiting here without word from Scar. She had to do something.

"Come," Sarabi told Kito. "It is time I make a decision."

"Finally," her sister said.

Sarabi shot her a scathing look.

"I'm sorry," Kito quickly added.

She and Kito made their way over to where the others were all sitting with their cubs. Fayola had not allowed Abena or Ola to move more than a few feet from her since the younger cub's return. To think of how much they had all secretly derided Sarafina over her overprotectiveness of Nala these past six months… Fayola had quickly begun to mirror her behaviour.

It occurred to Sarabi that she had not seen Sarafina in quite some time. She scanned those gathered here but did not see her amongst the lionesses. Goodness, she hoped she had not taken off on her own.

"Where is Scar?" Sefu asked the moment Sarabi reached them. "He should be back with Nala by now."

"I know we are all very concerned," Sarabi said. "I am, too, of course. But we all heard what Scar said."

"He—"

"But—"

Sarabi put up a paw, silencing them.

"However," she continued, "sitting by and doing nothing while Nala continues to get further and further away is more than any of us can bear. Therefore, I have come to a decision."

A hum of expectation began to rumble through the lionesses.

"The new moon arrives in two days' time," Sarabi said. "If Scar is not back with Nala by then, I will dispatch teams to go in search of both of them.

"We have to wait two days?" Thandi asked. "Anything can happen in that time."

"It is an act of outright defiance to go at all," Sarabi reminded her. "If Scar questions my motives, I will tell him that I feared there was an accident." Sarabi released an uneasy breath. "I would hope that Zazu would come back with word if Scar did indeed have an accident before he found Nala, but anything can happen out there in the jungle."

"Especially when our so-called leader is completely unqualified to do the job."

"Thandi," Sarabi said in a warning tone.

"She is right and you know it," Sefu said. "We never

should have entrusted Nala's safety to Scar."

"Did you have a choice?" Sarabi asked. "Did any of us? I do not have to remind any of you that there are laws in this kingdom. If you do not wish to abide by them, then you do not want to be part of this pride."

There was a collective gasp.

Her words were harsh, but necessary. She had to maintain order amongst them.

"Have I made myself clear?" Sarabi asked.

Their displeasure was tangible, but they all nodded their agreement.

The lionesses dispersed, returning to their cubs. Thandi and Kito walked over to the outcropping so they could lie in the sun and nap. Olee, ever the one to want to ease tension around Pride Rock, asked some of the cubs to join her in a game of hide-and-seek.

But there was one lioness missing.

Sarabi looked around until her eyes finally landed on Sarafina. She sat clear across the water hole, on the side where the zebras and gazelles usually gathered. She sat with her back to the water, staring out towards the Shadowlands.

Sarabi closed her eyes against the deep hurt that slashed through her. She knew what it was like to stare out into the distance, wondering if your cub was out there somewhere. To wonder if they were safe, if they would ever return to you.

Sarabi knew what it was like to grab hold of every single crumb of hope one could find and cling to it like nothing else mattered in life. Because nothing else did.

She ached to go to her, but for the first time in her life, Sarabi wasn't sure if her friend would welcome her. Her pain deepened. This rift between herself and Sarafina was something she could never have predicted. They had been inseparable their entire lives, but at this very moment, they seemed a thousand miles apart.

She thought back to the argument and Sarafina's horrible, hurtful words. Sarabi waited for the anger to reappear, but it never emerged. Instead, she felt... understanding. Now that the shocking ache had worn off, she was able to put herself in Sarafina's paw prints. Because she had walked in them herself. She understood why her friend had said the things she'd said. She had been so overprotective of Nala because she didn't want to go through the heartache of losing a cub, the way Sarabi had. Who would?

Yet, here Sarafina was, going through the one thing she had done her best to avoid all these months.

Sarabi took a tentative step forwards, then another. She continued, moving slowly, giving herself time to think through what she wanted to say.

But when she arrived at Sarafina's side, she could not think of a single word that would ease her friend's pain.

Everything seemed inadequate.

Sarabi quietly settled alongside Sarafina. She stared straight ahead, looking in the same direction her friend did. Then she reached over and tentatively set her paw upon Sarafina's.

She felt the other lioness stiffen and was sure she would jerk her paw away. But then Sarafina settled her chin against Sarabi's neck and began to weep.

Sarabi held herself up as strong and firm as possible, bearing Sarafina's weight.

Words were never spoken, because words were unnecessary.

CHAPTER TWENTY-FOUR

Nala never saw it coming.

One minute she was wending her way along the spongy forest floor, taking in the extraordinary sights around her, and the next she was tumbling like a rock down the side of a mountain, felled by a thick tree root that jutted from the ground. She yelped, barrelling headlong until she came to a stop. It wasn't until she opened her eyes that she realised what had stopped her.

Scar's paw.

He peered down at her, that scar above his eye arching with his cynical stare.

"Do you think rolling will get you to Garamba faster than walking?"

"I tripped on a tree root," Nala said, embarrassment heating her face.

Zazu swooped in, his wings flapping. "Miss Nala, are you okay? That was an awful fall."

"I'm fine," Nala said, pushing herself up on all fours. She gingerly shook her head to clear it. An ache from where a branch had struck her during her unfortunate excursion with those monkeys still throbbed just above her eye. At least her leg wasn't hurting as much anymore. And the cut she'd suffered during her trek through the Elephant Graveyard with Abena hadn't reopened. She sure was racking up the battle wounds on this adventure.

"I warned you that the jungle can be a dangerous place," Zazu said in that annoyingly superior voice of his. "You must be more careful."

What she needed to do was keep her eyes focused on moving forwards, but she was too mesmerised by the lush forest to pay attention to potential hazards. She couldn't take three steps without looking up at the trees stretching high into the sky.

The land was ornamented with thousands of brightly coloured flowers, the yellow and pink and violet blooms emitting a sweet-smelling aroma that wrapped itself around her. It was unlike anything she had ever seen around Pride Rock, where a few lilies would pop up from time to time near the water hole, and during the wet season, if they were lucky, they might see a daisy here and there. But nothing like this.

Zazu had explained that the closer they got to Garamba, the denser the vegetation would become. After months and months of drought at home, the rich, abundant blooms here were more than Nala could have ever hoped for.

If Simba really had been in Garamba all this time, Nala would be hard-pressed to forgive him for not returning to Pride Rock, but she would understand. She wouldn't want to leave this either.

And they hadn't even made it to Garamba yet. How much *more* beautiful could it be *there*?

"Are you able to walk, or will I have to carry you the rest of the way?" Scar now asked her.

"No, no, I can walk," Nala said hastily. She refused to become a burden, especially to Scar. Nala couldn't shake the sense that something was off with him.

It had taken a little convincing on her part, but Scar had seemed receptive to her reasoning as to why she thought Simba was in Garamba. Maybe it was the mention of Rafiki's vision that persuaded him. He appeared to be as eager to find Simba as she was.

Yet, something in her gut told her to keep her guard up and her eyes and ears open. Nala wasn't sure if the distrust the other lionesses felt towards their leader had somehow rubbed off on her or what, but she knew that she shouldn't ignore her instincts.

Guilt prickled at the back of her neck. Maybe she was being unfair to Scar. He was, after all, helping her continue her search for Simba when he could have demanded they head back to Pride Rock after he had saved her from the monkeys.

Nala glanced up at him. That uneasy feeling refused to go away. She couldn't brush it aside even if she wanted to.

They continued their trek through the jungle, and as Zazu had predicted, the further they walked, the thicker the vegetation became. Branches slapped at her head as Nala tried to navigate the narrow gaps between trees. It was a good thing Scar knew where he was going, because even if the stars *were* out tonight, Nala would not have been able to see them through the canopy of dense leaves overhead.

"Do you know how many different animal species there are in this part of Africa?" Zazu asked.

Nala suppressed a sigh. This journey would be a lot more enjoyable if Zazu would stop with all the questions.

"Miss Nala? Miss Nala!" he called.

"Yes, Zazu?" Nala replied.

"I asked if you know how many different animal species there are in this part of Africa," he repeated.

"Five hundred million," she said.

"Oh, come now. That was not a serious answer. How many—"

"Speaking of animal species," Scar interrupted. "I am famished after that tussle with those macaques. I think we should take a short break while you hunt, Nala."

Nala gulped. "You want *me* to hunt down food? For all of us?" she asked.

"I wasn't talking to the wind, child."

Maybe he hadn't heard the news around Pride Rock regarding her skills in that arena.

"I'm not very good at hunting," Nala said, then quickly added, "but I am getting better at it. I caught a baby hare earlier today."

"A baby hare is a snack, Nala. I need a gazelle, at the very least."

"A gazelle?"

Was he serious?

"How hard can it be?" Scar asked.

If it was so easy, why didn't he do it?

Hmm… that wasn't such a bad idea. If she and Scar teamed up, the two of them could corner their prey the way she and Abena had.

"Would you be willing to help me hunt?"

"Oh, Nala. Hunting is for lionesses."

"Well, I'm only a lion cub," she pointed out. "But maybe if we put together one grown lion and one lion cub, it will equal a lioness. Maybe."

"Clever," Scar said.

"Come on, Scar," Nala said. "This should be fun."

"Fun is taking a nap with the sun beaming down on me after I've eaten a nice meal provided by my pride's lionesses," Scar said. He rolled his eyes and released an exaggeratedly irritated breath. "But I guess I have to work for my food, in addition to rescuing you. Come on."

For all his complaining, Scar turned out to be a better hunter than Nala had first imagined. He still didn't measure up to the lionesses in their pride. Neither of them did, which was why they'd had to settle for a small aardwolf as their dinner.

Zazu had thankfully gone off to forage for his own dinner, so Nala was spared from having to listen to him blabber on about how many species of insects existed in the world, or other such nonsense. She and Scar ate in relative silence, and then Scar sprawled out along a fallen tree trunk and yawned.

"Although the meal was rather paltry, I still need time to digest it before we continue," he said. He seared her with a withering stare. "There will be no repeats of your previous foolishness, because I will not chase down a pack of raging monkeys to save you again."

"Okay, okay," Nala said. It wasn't as if she had set out to get cub-napped.

But the moment Scar shut his eyes, an idea began to take root in Nala's mind.

This was supposed to be her big adventure, but she had yet to hunt a meal on her own. Abena had tracked down the hare they'd eaten the first night, and she couldn't really count the one she had caught on her own. It was too small to feed a two-day-old cub. She'd joined up with Scar on their hunt, but he had done most of the work.

She wanted to finally be the one to bring in the kill, all on her own. And she was determined to capture something that was bigger than herself this time.

Nala checked to make sure Scar was asleep. Not only was he sleeping, his rumbling snore was loud enough to scare away any potential prey. She would have to head a little further into the jungle.

She'd only taken two steps when Zazu appeared in front of her.

"Ah, ah, ah, young lady. Just where do you think you're going?"

"Shhh," Nala said, nodding towards Scar. "I'm not running away this time. I promise."

"I'm not so sure your promises mean anything anymore, missy."

Nala gritted her teeth. Zazu and his loud mouth were going to ruin this for her.

"Psst." She jerked her head towards a sugarbush. Once behind it, she told him, "I'm not leaving. I'm going to hunt."

"Didn't you just eat? Granted, the little aardwolf wasn't very big, but it looked sufficient enough to me. Of course, I'm not like you carnivores."

Nala rolled her eyes. "Zazu, can I go now?"

"Hmm, let me get His Majesty to accompany you."

"No!" she said louder than she had anticipated. Nala looked back at the log where Scar slept, then returned her attention to Zazu. "I don't want Scar's help. All the cubs back at Pride Rock have hunted on their own, except for me. I want to prove that I can do this by myself. Just let me do this, Zazu."

He studied her with that assessing stare for so long that Nala feared he would reject her plea. But then his expression softened and he nodded. "Okay, Miss Nala. But be careful."

"I will," Nala said, excitement rushing through her.

She took a moment to survey the area, cataloguing the landmarks so that she could find her way back, then she set out for the most obvious place to find prey: a water hole. But she had only travelled a few yards when she caught movement out of the corner of her eye. Nala whipped her head around.

An impala.

It stood about six paces away, munching on grass shoots. It wasn't a gazelle, but it would do just fine. Nala took a step towards it and the animal's ears perked up. She froze.

The impala looked from side to side, sniffing the air. Nala held her breath, afraid to make even the slightest sound. A wave of relief rushed over her when the animal returned to its meal.

Unbidden, the taunts of the other cubs began to play in her head. She could hear their teasing and jeering as if they were right here with her. She could hear her mother yelling for her to return to her side.

Nala pushed it all out of her mind. She wouldn't allow the doubts to hold her back this time.

She slowed her breathing and concentrated, keeping the impala in her sights. She squatted, using the tall shoots and reeds for cover, then she pounced. She clamped her teeth on the impala's neck just as Abena had instructed her, and in a matter of minutes, she had the animal completely subdued. Nala smiled even as she continued to hold down the impala.

She'd done it!

She was so giddy she became light-headed. Excitement and relief expanded in her chest, the emotion overwhelming her. She had done it! She'd proved she could be an asset to her pride, that they could rely on her, despite how much her mum's overprotectiveness had held her back.

She dropped the carcass and spun around in a circle.

"I did it!" Nala yelped. "I did it! I did it! I did it!"

She clamped her jaw on her kill's hind leg and tugged. The impala barely moved.

She'd managed to capture it, but dragging it back to where Scar slept wouldn't be so easy. Nala hoped he didn't mind her waking him, because there was no way she was leaving her first big kill here for others to enjoy.

She ran back to where Scar was still stretched out along the tree.

"Scar! Zazu! Come quick!" she called. She pushed at Scar with her paws.

He lifted one eyelid and snarled at her. "This had better be—" He stopped. "What is that on your face? Is that—"

Nala wiped at her face and came away with blood. "I killed an impala," she said with a grin.

Scar jerked his head back in surprise and rose from the downed tree.

"Very impressive, young Nala. Show me. I've been ready to feast on some real food."

She guided Scar to the spot and was relieved to find her kill right where she'd left it.

"Very impressive indeed," Scar said as they came upon

the carcass. "And you thought you weren't a hunter. It looks to me like you'll make a fine hunter for the pride."

Nala beamed at his praise. She couldn't help it.

They enjoyed their dinner, leaving what they could not finish for other animals that might be around and in need of a meal.

Now that he had napped, Scar decided he was ready to continue on their journey. He asked Nala if she needed to rest, but she was still too excited about her successful hunt to even think about sleep.

"Good," Scar told her. "If we push through the rest of the night, we should arrive in Garamba by midday."

Midday. She was less than a day from possibly seeing Simba again. Between that realisation and the exhilaration of her kill, Nala felt as if she were floating.

She looked up at Scar. Maybe she had misjudged him. When she thought about their time together, she had to admit that he had done nothing to warrant any misgivings. Could it be that the lionesses back at Pride Rock just hadn't given Scar a fair chance?

"You know, Scar, you're not as bad as the other lionesses make you out to be," Nala said. "Maybe if you came down to the water hole when the rest of us are there, they would get to know you better."

"Oh, really?" Scar drawled.

"Young Nala is right, Sire," Zazu said. "We could use less tension around Pride Rock."

"Well," Scar said, "maybe when we return, you can put in a good word for me."

The scar above his eye contracted with his knowing wink.

CHAPTER TWENTY-FIVE

The thunder started soon after they passed the huge downed tree where Scar had first stopped. The low rumble had become a familiar sound over the last three days. Nala knew Pride Rock desperately needed the rain – she'd heard her mother, Sarabi and the other lionesses discussing it enough – but *she* certainly didn't need any more of it slowing her down.

"Another storm?" Zazu asked. "My, I guess the drought is over."

"I would say so," Scar said. He squinted up at the sky as if trying to look between the tree branches. "We should still continue on, at least until we get to Mount Kei. Once there, we can rest until the storm passes." Scar peered down at her. "I could use some sleep."

He was probably right. She hadn't felt tired when they'd first started out again, but after the excitement of hunting the impala began to wear off, the fatigue had slammed into her. She hoped this Mount Kei wasn't too far. If she slowed them down too much, she feared she would start to look like a baby again in Scar's and Zazu's eyes. She'd come too far to let that happen.

Even as the wind picked up, a heaviness settled in the air. Nala had experienced this before.

"I don't think we'll make it to that mountain before the" – a fat raindrop plopped on her nose – "rain," she finished. A few more drops pitter-pattered around them, but it was nothing compared to the previous storm she and Abena had faced.

"This isn't so bad," Zazu said. "Maybe we can—"

Before he could get the rest of the words out, the skies cracked open and the rain became blinding, pounding the earth with a violence Nala had never seen before.

"Oh my!" Zazu said. "We must find shelter."

A streak of lightning struck the ground just a few feet from them. Nala screamed.

"Over there," Scar said. He caught Nala by her scruff and took off at full speed towards a rock formation that was bigger than the kopje where she and Abena had taken shelter, but not as big as Pride Rock. They huddled underneath a slab that jutted out from the rock. It shook with every clap of thunder, showering them with rocky pebbles and dust.

"In all my years I have never witnessed such storms before," Zazu said. "It is at times like this that I wish Rafiki were around. He would have answers to what is going on with this peculiar weather."

"If it is anything like the last storm, it will not last long," Scar said. "Let us be grateful we found a place to wait it out."

Nala was grateful for both the shelter and the companionship. A shudder raced through her as she imagined what it would have been like to be out here in this jungle alone while this storm raged.

Zazu continued to prattle on about the change in the intensity of the storms compared to when he was a young bird. Nala tuned him out when he moved on to the severity of the drought. Fatigue was setting in, and as much as she tried to fight it, her exhaustion was winning.

Her head lolled to the side and she stumbled against Scar's leg. "Sorry," Nala said, quickly righting herself. She stood up straight, but only seconds later felt herself listing again.

"Go to sleep, Nala," Scar said.

"No… I—"

"Go to sleep," Scar said again.

Nala didn't object a second time. She nestled against the side of the rock and rested her chin on her paws. Thunder continued to roar in the distance, but it was now far enough away not to scare her. The rain still poured, but it lacked the fervour of a few minutes ago. It was actually pleasant, lulling her to sleep with its melodic *thump, thump, thump*.

She wasn't sure how long she'd napped when her sleep was interrupted by a sneering voice.

"What do we have here?"

Nala's head popped up. She whipped around.

Three lions, all with full bouffant manes, stood a few yards back, just at the edge of the overhang. Nala saw Scar stiffen. Clouds obscured the moon, which made it even more difficult to see the lions' faces, but Nala could already tell by the tone of the one who'd spoken that this welcome wouldn't be a warm one.

"Well, if it isn't Scar," the lion in the middle said.

"Hello, Akeem," Scar replied, his voice as calm and cool as ever.

"Never thought I'd see you again," the lion said. "Oh, wait. It's not that I never *thought* I'd see you again, it's that I never *wanted* to see you again. In fact, I warned you never to show your face around here, Scar."

Nala could hear her heartbeat pounding in her ears. She scooted to the side until she stood underneath Scar.

"We don't want any trouble," Scar said.

"Oh no? So why are you in Hatari territory? You know you're not welcome here."

Who were the Hatari? And what could Scar have possibly done to get banished from their territory?

"Gentlemen, please," Scar said. "Any past disagreements have no place here. We are only passing through on our way to Garamba. As you see, I have a young cub with me."

"So, is that what you do now? Bring a cub on your little outings so that you can hide behind him?" asked the one Scar had called Akeem.

"She looks like a girl cub to me," the burly lion on the right said. "You getting little girl cubs to fight your battles, Scar?"

"There will be no fighting," Scar said. He sounded calm, but Nala could feel his heart beating from where she stood underneath him. It pounded as frantically as her own.

If Scar was afraid, they were in trouble.

The lions advanced. Scar took a step back. Nala did the same.

"Gentlemen, stand down," Scar said in the authoritative voice that usually got the lionesses' attention. It had no effect on the three lions stalking towards them.

She surreptitiously glanced around for Zazu, but he was nowhere. He must have flown off while she had been napping.

"The last time you were here, we told you if you ever set foot on Hatari land again, you were a goner. Mufasa isn't here to save you this time. And it looks like your little bodyguard isn't up for the job either."

The lion that had not spoken yet looked at Nala.

"Go," he said to her.

Nala huddled closer to Scar.

"You better listen to him, little cubby," the other lion said. "He usually eats cubs like you for a snack."

"Gentlemen, please," Scar said, taking yet another step back. "This has been blown out of proportion. We made an honest mistake. It has been such a long time since I have been around these parts; I didn't remember the boundary of your territory. Surely, you have made such mistakes yourself, Akeem."

"Your mistake was not sending this little cub away, because now you're both going to be dinner," Akeem said.

Nala gasped. Were they really preparing to kill them?

"You don't want to feed on an old lion like me," Scar said. "I've been around for far too long. I'm probably rancid underneath all this fur."

Nala looked up at him. What about her? Why wasn't he

telling them all the reasons they wouldn't want to eat *her*?

"There's only one way to find out," the burly lion said to Scar. He shot Nala a terrifying scowl. "Go, before I make a cub sandwich out of you."

She heard Scar sigh. "Leave, Nala," he said.

"No!" Nala said.

She couldn't leave him. If she did, these lions would tear him apart.

What was she thinking? They would tear him apart even if she stayed. The only difference is that they would tear *her* apart too. She was no match for these lions.

"Nala, I said leave," Scar told her.

No!

This was not how her adventure would end. Scar's death would not be the reason their pride gained a new king. She, Simba *and* Scar were all going to return to Pride Rock safely. They had to.

The three lions moved in.

"You'd better get out of here, cub," Akeem said. "This has nothing to do with you."

They were aiming to kill her king. This had everything to do with her!

But she was one small cub, and all three of the lions appeared to be younger and stronger than Scar. The odds were not in his favour.

"Nala, leave. I won't say it again."

"Yeah, leave," the burly lion said.

She turned to Scar and recoiled at the lack of concern she saw in his eyes. He seemed to have given up. He knew he was cornered. It would take a miracle to save him, but he didn't have a miracle; all he had was her.

And she…

She wasn't giving up. Not yet. The old Nala would have cowered in fear, but she had gone through too much in her quest to find Simba. She would not allow these ruffians to ruin it all.

She couldn't fight them, but she could do *some*thing. She had to figure out some way to get them out of this mess.

Nala turned and pleaded with the three lions. "Please, let him go. You don't understand. We're on an important mis—"

"Nala!" Scar yelled. "Get out of here right now!"

"You better listen to him, Nala," Akeem said.

She started moving away from the advancing lions. They were done listening to her. And if she didn't get out of here soon, she might become their next meal.

She turned to Scar. "I'm sorry," she said. Then she turned to the trio. "Fine. I'll leave."

But she was not giving up.

CHAPTER TWENTY-SIX

Scar affected an air of indifference, nonchalantly picking at the dirt underneath his claws. Internally, his entire being quaked with fear. The rain must have altered both his sight and his thinking, because he never would have knowingly wandered into Hatari territory. He had learnt his lesson the last time he'd found himself here.

Back then, he'd had Mufasa's brawn to assist in getting him out of the pickle he'd got himself into with the Hatari pride, but thanks to him, his brother wasn't at his side this time.

Here were those unforeseen consequences of his actions rearing their ugly heads again. It could not have come at a more inopportune time.

Think! Scar chastised himself.

He was a talker. Surely, he could talk his way out of this.

"Okay, gentlemen," Scar said. He held up both paws. "Now that you've scared off the cub with your menacing scowls – those scowls have got better, by the way – can we handle this like adults?"

"Oh, you think that was a show for the cub?" Akeem asked, closing the distance between them. "Do we look like travelling troubadours to you?"

Should he tell him that troubadours were songwriters and not actors? Probably not.

Scar also decided against telling Akeem that they looked like they could all use a good bath. Voicing his opinion on that subject would only lead to an earlier death. Hakim appeared to be on the brink of charging at him right this moment. The meathead lion had never liked him, and that was even *before* Scar had tried to exert dominance over their little pride back when Hakim was its sole ruler. Now that his two brothers had returned to the fold, they were even bigger bullies.

Maybe if Scar's brother had allowed him to share the leadership duties in their pride, Scar would not have gone out looking for another pride to rule. So it was Mufasa's fault. Mufasa may have got him out of trouble with the Hatari all those years ago, but it had been because of Mufasa that Scar had got into that trouble in the first place.

And this time his trouble was all due to Mufasa's son. It was so ironic, he would laugh if his current situation weren't so dire.

He should have returned to Pride Rock when he'd found Nala sleeping in that first kopje. Instead, his bloodlust for Simba was going to get him killed.

Maybe *he* was the troubadour here. Scar could not think of anything more tragically poetic than the tale of his impending demise.

"Hope that little cub knows the way back home," Akeem said as he and Hakim broke away from their brother, approaching Scar from opposite sides. "Because you won't be able to show her how to get there."

"Gentlemen," Scar said. He retreated until his back slammed against the wall at the base of the rock formation. "This is quite unnecessary. I did not invade your territory on purpose. Like I told you, it was an honest mistake. I had to get the cub out of the rain."

They continued advancing. The third brother – Scar couldn't even remember his name – snarled, baring teeth so sharp that he could already feel them sinking into his flesh.

"There must be something I can do to make this up to you three," he said. "There's no need for bloodshed."

Just then, several pebbles fell from the sky, landing behind Akeem. Scar covertly peered up and noticed two tiny white cub paws curled over the edge of the overhang.

Nala poked her head out and pointed to the right.

Scar glanced out of the corner of his eye. That's when he saw it: a sliver of an opening between two boulders. It had been behind him before the lions had backed him against the wall. Combined with the clouds obscuring the moonlight, it was no wonder he'd missed it.

But how was he supposed to make it to that opening?

Suddenly a loud caw sounded from high above. Scar's eyes bulged in astonishment as Zazu charged in from the ledge where Nala had been a moment ago and clipped Akeem on the head. Chaos erupted amongst the three lions as Zazu zigzagged through the air, taking aim at each of them.

Scar used the distraction just as that smart Nala had intended. He inched to the right, then raced past the trio of lions who were still fighting with Zazu. He squeezed through the opening and into the clearing that surrounded the rock formation.

"Scar! This way!"

"That was genius, Nala," Scar said as he ran up alongside her.

"We can talk about my genius later. We need to get to the other side of that river. That's where the Hatari territory ends. They can't touch you once you cross the river."

"I knew that, but how did you?"

"Zebras," she called over her shoulder. "I asked a few who were running past here on their way to the Pemba Forest."

She really was a genius.

Scar captured her by the scruff of her neck and sprinted towards the narrow river that lay ahead.

"Run, Sire!" Zazu appeared at his side, coursing through the air like lightning. "Run! Run! Run!"

Scar didn't even pause at the bank of the river; he dived in, carrying Nala with him. He knew it to be both narrow and shallow from the times he'd come to this region in the past.

One thing he had not expected was the swiftness of the current. The heavy rains had caused the river to swell more than usual, sending him and Nala sailing south.

It was to their advantage; Scar looked back and saw the three male Hatari lions running along the bank of the river, but they couldn't keep up with the speed that he and Nala travelled. The rock formation where they'd taken shelter grew smaller and smaller. Zazu continued flying just above them. He yelled out warnings, instructing Scar about what to look out for in the water.

Once they reached a spot Scar was certain was no longer in Hatari territory, he sought out a branch that he could grab to lift them out of the river. He saw a thick one hanging over the bank just up ahead.

Scar waited until they were just below it and then reached up. Hauling them out of the river, he scooted along the underside of the heavy low-hanging branch. Once they'd made it to safety, he dropped Nala from his jaws then promptly collapsed on the bank of the river, giving in to the exhaustion his escape had wrought.

Scar sucked in deep breaths, filling his lungs with much-needed air. He could not believe he was alive.

"My word, Sire. That was treacherous," Zazu said, landing next to Scar's head.

"Where… Nala?" Scar asked.

"I'm here," he heard her call.

Scar found the strength to turn so that he could see for himself. Her drenched fur was slick against her face, but she looked no worse for the wear.

"Nala, that… that was… that was very stupid," Scar said. "Brave, but stupid."

She grimaced. "Thanks. I think."

"It was more brave than stupid, in my opinion, Miss Nala," Zazu said. "How very smart to come up with that distraction. Of course, it helped that those lions were not the brightest fireflies in the forest, if you know what I mean." The bird tapped the side of his head. "But I must give credit where credit is due. You formed a brilliant plan, and it worked out perfectly. The pride would be so proud of you."

Nala beamed. "Thanks, Zazu! I'm proud of me too."

"I didn't say I wasn't proud of you," Scar said. "But you put yourself in grave danger."

For him.

Scar wasn't sure how to feel. Nala could have left him – she *should* have left him. The minute Akeem and his brothers had allowed her to leave, she should have taken off for home, or continued on to Garamba if that was what she wanted. No matter what, she should not have stayed to help him.

Yet, she had. No one had ever made such a sacrifice for him. For it to have been made by one so young... her bravery took away what little breath he still had.

"Why didn't you just leave?" Scar asked her.

"Well..." She hesitated for a moment, dipping her head. When she looked up at him, there was gratitude in her eyes. "You saved my life. I thought it was only fair I do whatever I could to save yours."

It suddenly became painful to swallow. Scar didn't recognise the emotions this bedraggled little cub had stirred within him, and he wasn't sure he wanted to recognise them. He steered clear of emotion, especially those that made him feel indebted to anyone.

Indebted?

He stuck his nose in the air.

He wasn't indebted to Nala. He hadn't asked her to rescue him; she had decided to do so on her own.

"Oh, bother," Scar muttered.

That attitude usually worked for him, but it would appear that his dormant conscience had decided to make its presence known. He simply could not downplay Nala's courageous act.

"In case I did not say it before…" He knew he had not said it before. "Thank you," he finished with a begrudged huff.

She turned her smile to him.

"Anytime, Scar. Anytime."

CHAPTER TWENTY-SEVEN

Nala's eyes popped open.

A wide smile broke out across her face as excitement hummed from the ends of her paws to the tips of her ears.

She didn't need Zazu to wake her up this time. The anticipation zipping through her veins was more than enough to do the job. She pushed herself up and stretched her front legs out in front of her, feeling refreshed and ready after much-needed rest.

The plan had been to make it past Mount Kei, but according to Scar, their sail down the river after their run-in with the Hatari pride had taken them too far away from the mountain to get there before they would need to sleep. Nala hadn't wanted to say anything at the time, but she'd nearly cried with relief when he suggested they hunker down for a few hours in a cave not far from the river. She had been so exhausted that she could barely stay upright.

But now she was wide awake and ready for what today promised to bring: Simba! She was going to see Simba!

Not so fast!

She had to tamp down her excitement. She had warned herself from the very outset of this mission that finding Simba was not a guarantee. The reported sighting could turn out to be nothing more than a disappointing case of mistaken identity, just as all the others had been up to this point. She could not lose sight of that.

Yet, Nala also could not ignore the feeling tingling in her gut that told her this was real, that Simba was alive, and that she was going to bring him home.

But she had to find him first.

She dashed over to where Scar lay against the wall, his snores echoing around the entire cave.

"Wake up!" Nala said, pushing at him with both paws. Scar had told her before they settled in for the night that if they left at dawn, they should arrive in Garamba well before the sunset.

"The sun is coming up," Nala said. "It's time to go."

Scar let out a loud yawn and smacked his lips. He lifted one eyelid, growled and sighed. "Why are cubs always so noisy?"

"Come on, Scar. We have to get going."

Another sigh. "My body is not used to all this activity. Hunting for my own food, escaping a trio of numbskulls; it's all too much."

"Scar," Nala said with an exasperated sigh of her own. "We're almost to Garamba. You said it yourself. Let's go! It's time to find Simba and bring him back to Pride Rock!"

He opened both eyes at the mention of Simba. "You're right," Scar said. "That's the reason for all this, isn't it? To find my nephew."

"And bring him home!" Nala said. "Now, where is Zazu? It's time for us to go."

He must have heard his name, because the majordomo flew into the cave at that precise moment, a worm dangling from his beak.

"Well, good morning!" Zazu exclaimed after swallowing down the worm. Yuck. "I am happy to report that the weather looks wonderful. Not a cloud in the sky. It should be smooth sailing to Garamba. But, hopefully, no sailing down rivers this time. I think we have had enough of that."

"Might I suggest a game," Scar said as he executed the same stretch Nala had. "No talking until we reach Garamba. Doesn't that sound like fun?"

"No," Nala and Zazu said at the same time.

Scar rolled his eyes. "Fine. Let us be on our way."

Nala didn't need any further prompting. She dashed out of the cave, ecstatic to see that Zazu had not exaggerated about the weather. There would be no storms slowing them down today.

The sunny skies did nothing to brighten Scar's mood, but Nala was coming to accept that this was just how he was. She had to admit that she was grateful to have him by her side as they set off for this last leg of their trip. She was even grateful for Zazu, although she wished he would play Scar's 'no talking' game for a while.

It was funny when she thought about it. When she first came up with the idea of searching for Simba, she was determined to do it all on her own, which was why she had been reluctant to let Abena follow her the night she'd sneaked away from Pride Rock. Yet, the younger cub had proved to be a great asset. Not only had Nala appreciated her companionship – she had relied on Abena for her hunting skills.

And here she was experiencing that same appreciation for Scar.

As she'd managed to get kidnapped by a pack of macaques during the only portion of her journey that she *had* travelled alone, she was lucky to have had Abena, Scar and Zazu by her side.

It got her to thinking: maybe she should have told

others about her plans from the very beginning. It wasn't the first time this thought had popped into her head since setting out on this journey. If she had shared what she knew with Sarabi, their queen would have dispatched the senior lionesses and they probably would have reached Garamba by now.

They probably would have been on their way back to Pride Rock with Simba already!

And that's what this was all about, wasn't it? Finding Simba.

Nala pressed her lips together as an unsettling realisation forced her to face an upsetting truth. She had been thinking more about herself when she first set out on this journey, and less about her friend. She'd wanted to prove to her pride – and especially to her mother – that she could do this on her own.

But at what cost?

She had nearly got herself killed. Worse, she had almost got Scar killed as well.

This was supposed to be about Simba. It was about her pride's future. Instead, she had selfishly made it all about her.

She owed everyone in her pride a huge apology. Nala knew where she could start.

"Scar?" She waited for him to look at her. "I'm sorry."

"It's fine, Nala. I had to wake up eventually," he said.

"No, I mean I'm sorry that you had to come out here to find me, and I'm sorry for making the pride worry. Even though it was for a good reason," she quickly added. "But it was also selfish. I especially should have told Sarabi about Simba's plans to visit Garamba after the mongoose said that he had been spotted there."

"Oh, don't worry about Sarabi," Scar said. "She will be so happy to see Simba that it won't matter that you kept such an enormous secret from her all this time."

When he put it that way…

Nala ran up ahead of him and started to walk backwards so that she could face him. "At least my intentions were honourable," she tried.

"Of course," Scar said. "We all have good intentions, dear. We just sometimes make stupid choices."

"Like saving your life?" she reminded him. She shouldn't really throw that in his face since she was the reason he'd been put in that position in the first place. Before he could bring up that fact, she quickly added, "Also, my mum says it isn't nice to call anyone stupid. And I wouldn't say I made a stupid choice. It was just… unwise. But I've learnt from it."

"And that is what is important, that you learn from your mistakes," Zazu piped in. "I say it all the time. One can make a mistake, but one must learn from it."

Nala had never heard him say anything like that before.

"Well, I would suggest that you make even better choices in the future," Scar said. "Like making sure you don't walk into a tree."

Nala turned around just before bumping into one of the biggest trees she had ever seen in her life. She followed Scar around it, and then stopped short.

"Wow," Nala whispered.

They stood at the edge of what could only be described as paradise.

Scar stuck his chest out as if he had created what lay before them and said, "Welcome to Garamba."

CHAPTER TWENTY-EIGHT

"We made it," Nala said in an awed voice, unable to take her eyes off the wondrous sights that lay before her.

Everything was so green and lush. Trees of every size and height grew so close together that it was hard to tell where one stopped and the next one started. Thick, ropey vines connected them, draping from one to another.

A waterfall cascaded down the grass-covered slope of a mountain, spilling into a basin with the bluest water she had ever seen. A rainbow – a real rainbow – arced over the basin.

Garamba was everything she and Simba had imagined it would be, and more.

Simba.

Was he here? Had he been living in this dreamland all this time? She had to find out.

"We need to find Simba," Nala said. But before she could take off, Scar stopped her, pinning her tail under his paw.

"Not so fast. Garamba is vast. And you have no idea where Simba is. He could be anywhere."

"If he's here, he is at the Blue Grotto," Nala said confidently. "We just have to find it." She tried to move forwards, but Scar still held her.

"Of the three of us, only one has been to Garamba," he said. "You will follow my lead. This jungle is beautiful, but it is still a jungle and there are pitfalls everywhere. Now, follow me."

Nala ached to break away from him and go in search of the Blue Grotto on her own, but Scar was right. There were probably dangers lurking all around this amazing place. She hadn't come this far only to fall into quicksand or stumble upon a snake pit. It was better to let him lead.

As she followed Scar, Nala soon realised that she would not have got very far on her own anyway because she couldn't walk five steps without stopping to take in the incredible sights of the jungle. They travelled along a narrow trail of trampled leaves. On either side stood those massive trees that seemed tall enough to touch the sky. But she couldn't see the sky because the leaves and vines were so abundant that they created a canopy over their heads.

The foliage covering the ground was as thick as the leaves above. And it was everywhere! Even on the trees!

"I've never seen grass growing on the sides of trees before," Nala said.

"It's moss. We have moss on the trees back in the savanna," Scar said.

"Not like this," Nala replied. The moss that grew on the trees and rocks near Pride Rock was brown and stubby. This moss was as dense as the grass growing in the scrubland. Everything here was lush and verdant. She could tell in just the short time they had been here that Garamba was as remarkable as she and Simba had hoped it would be.

But where was Simba? Now that they were here, the need to find him thumped within her bones like a heartbeat.

"Scar, are you sure this is the way to the Blue Grotto?" she asked as she walked in step with him. She paused. "Wait. Is that water?"

She immediately took off, veering left of the path and heading towards the sound of gurgling water. She climbed over the protruding roots of the trees and underneath the wide, flat leaves of the foliage that grew everywhere.

"Nala, get back here!" she heard Scar yell, but she

kept going, not stopping until she reached the edge of a short cliff.

"Wow," Nala said as she released a low breath. Scar and Zazu quickly made it to her side, but Nala didn't acknowledge them. She couldn't tear her eyes away from the beauty on display.

At the base of the cliff was a stream with water so clear she could see the bed of smooth rocks that lay across the bottom of it. Fish of all sizes zipped through the stream, their myriad colours creating an underwater rainbow. It was all so vibrant – like nothing she had ever seen before.

Nala peered in the direction the fish swam. It suddenly occurred to her that this stream must lead to something. Maybe…

"Do you think this stream leads to the Blue Grotto?" she asked. She looked over at Scar. "Do you?"

"I can't be certain," Scar said. "It has been a long time since I've visited Garamba."

"But you said we had to follow you because you're the only one who's been here," she reminded him.

"Yes, well, it has changed. There were a lot fewer trees the last time I was here."

Nala barely managed to hold in her frustrated growl. "We should follow this stream," Nala said.

"Not so fast."

"But Scar!" she said.

He gave her one of those superior looks that challenged her to say another word. This time Nala *did* growl in frustration.

Scar scowled, but then he finally said, "We'll ask if any of the residents have seen Simba."

The moment they turned to go back to the trail, the sound of leaves rustling caught Nala's attention. She looked up at the trees just in front of them and saw a long-legged monkey swinging from one of the vines.

"Don't ask him," Nala said.

"That's a bonobo, Nala. They're harmless."

"He is right," Zazu said. "Do not let what happened with those macaques change the way you view all primates, Nala. They are not all out for blood."

Scar walked up to the tree where the monkey hung upside down, chomping on fruit of some sort.

"Excuse me," Scar said. "We're looking for a lion cub, about yay tall. Funny-shaped head."

Nala frowned up at him.

"Are you asking about Simba?" the bonobo asked.

Nala's heart stopped. "He's here?"

"Yeah." The bonobo took another bite of his fruit and chewed slowly. "Check the Blue Grotto," he finally continued. "He hangs out around there with Timon and Pumbaa."

He pointed in the direction the fish were swimming in the stream. "It's right that way, just past the waterfall."

He's here! Her pride's rightful king was here!

As tightly as she had held on to the hope of finding Simba alive, it wasn't until this very moment that Nala realised that deep within she had been secretly preparing herself for the opposite news. But she didn't have to fear awful news anymore, because Simba was here. He was alive!

She looked over at Scar. His mouth hung open. He looked as shocked as she felt.

"He's alive, Scar! Simba is alive! Let's go!"

She took off running towards the waterfall. Towards her best friend.

CHAPTER TWENTY-NINE

Scar followed Nala on shaky legs. His brain refused to comprehend the information that the bonobo had so casually shared.

Simba was alive.

Despite Rafiki's vision and Nala's insistence that, if alive, Simba would have travelled to Garamba, up until this point Scar never truly expected it to be true. He thought they would arrive and discover that this sighting had been like all the others reported over the last six months.

Zazu flew beside him, yammering excitedly about the miraculous news. Scar tuned him out, along with everything else. He could only focus on one thing: the fact that Mufasa's son still lived.

They walked past the waterfall before arriving at the opening of the sea cave, just as the monkey had instructed. Scar hung back, standing next to a rock pillar, while Nala continued forwards, taking slow, tentative steps as if afraid of what she would find. An air of anticipation swirled around them. Yet, it was eerily quiet, with only the sounds of the occasional primate squawking or bird cawing. Even Zazu was silent for once.

Nala crept closer to the opening of the grotto. Its rocky ledge appeared dangerously slick. It took every bit of restraint Scar had not to shove her in the water.

But he couldn't rid himself of Nala just yet, and especially not with Zazu as a witness. It was imperative that he be patient. Unlike those hyenas he'd first sent to do the job, Scar would make sure it was done the right way this time.

"Simba?" Nala called. His name echoed off the walls of the cave, but there was no response.

A spark of hope flickered in Scar's chest. Was it possible that the bonobo had been mistaken and Simba wasn't here after all?

But just as quickly as it had risen, his hope disintegrated with a single word, spoken in a voice that Scar had not heard in six months and one that he had been assured he would never hear again.

"Nala?"

Nala and Scar both turned at the same time.

There he was. Mufasa's spawn.

He stood with two others, a skinny meerkat and a plump warthog. It was exactly what Nala had recalled about Rafiki's vision.

Nala remained motionless for a moment, then she took off, screaming, "Simba!"

Scar watched with barely concealed contempt as the two embraced, jumping around in a circle. Zazu joined in the fray, hovering around the cubs with his wings flapping excitedly.

He should do it right now. Take them out one by one and be done with this for good.

But he couldn't. Not yet. He must get information from Simba; Scar had to know if the cub had discussed what happened to Mufasa with anyone else. Even Simba's incorrect version of events was too dangerous to leave out in the world. Anyone who had any knowledge of that day would need to be eliminated. It was the only way to secure his place as the leader of their kingdom.

"These are my friends, Timon and Pumbaa," Simba was saying to Nala. "They took me in when I got here to Garamba. I guess you can say they've become my family."

"Your family is back at Pride Rock," Nala said. "Your

mother will be so relieved to see you."

Simba's expression sobered at the mention of Sarabi. "How is she?" he asked.

"She misses you. Everyone misses you," Nala said. "I can't believe this, Simba. You're really here."

"I can't believe it either," Scar said, coming out from behind the pillar.

"Un— Uncle Scar," Simba said. Scar caught the way his body stiffened, and the apprehension he heard in the cub's voice was undeniable.

"Well, Simba," Scar said. "This is quite the surprise. How amazing to find you here in Garamba, just as that mongoose said you would be."

Scar had to hold in his smile. He could tell by the shocked terror in his nephew's eyes that his thoughts went directly to the day at the gorge. Had he figured out Scar's role in Mufasa's demise? Learning this was essential.

"You've been gone a long time, Simba," Scar said. "We all thought you had met some awful fate."

"Uh… no," Simba said. He dropped his head and stared at the ground.

"Simba, do you know about your father?" Nala asked in a cautious tone. "About what happened to him?"

His head shot up, his eyes going wide as he quickly glanced at Scar. "I know there was a stam— a stampede.

But I don't know what happened once the wildebeests left the gorge."

This time, Scar couldn't suppress his grin.

It was a lie. He knew exactly what had happened to his father. When Scar had discovered Simba, he had been huddled next to Mufasa's lifeless body.

There was only one reason Simba would share such a lie with Nala.

He still believed he had caused his father's death.

Scar should have known this was the case. It was why Simba's expression had gone from delighted to panic-stricken the moment he saw Scar.

Because Scar knew his secret.

And Simba was terrified that this deep, dark, horrible secret would be revealed now that he had been found.

"So, uh, you came with Uncle Scar?" Simba asked Nala.

"Yes. Well, first it was me and Abena, but then there was an elephant stampede and this raging storm, and both scared her so much that I had to take her back to Pride Rock. And she wasn't supposed to tell anyone where I was going, but you know she's just a cub so she couldn't keep her mouth shut. The next thing I knew, Scar and Zazu where there!"

On and on Nala went, recounting every part of her

journey to Simba. As she prattled on about how she'd swung through the trees with the macaques, Scar set out to devise a plan to rid himself of his nephew for good.

Now that he knew Simba had not figured out that Scar was the one behind Mufasa's death, he wondered if he could possibly use it to his advantage. He scratched at his jaw, trying to come up with a scenario that would lead to an accident for Simba, Nala and Zazu.

The most convenient way to go about this was to drown them, of course, but it would be too difficult to do it simultaneously. He would need to break them apart and take care of them one by one.

He had to start with Zazu.

Even though Scar felt as if he would explode if he did not get rid of his nephew first, Zazu was the one with the capability to ruin everything. If Zazu witnessed Scar harming Simba or Nala, Scar had no doubt the bird would fly back to Pride Rock and tell Sarabi everything. He had to be eliminated.

And then it was Simba's turn. Convincing his nephew to remain here in Garamba and not return to Pride Rock would not be good enough. He had to kill him.

But how? Simba would be overly cautious around Scar, knowing that Scar knew his secret. His nephew would probably watch him like a hawk, afraid Scar would let something slip in front of Nala or Zazu. Which would make it impossible to catch him unawares.

Unless…

Scar chuckled to himself. Why hadn't he thought of this earlier? He knew exactly how to catch Simba while his guard was down.

He walked up to where Simba, Nala and the others stood.

"Well, this little reunion is quite something, isn't it?" Scar said. "But, Nala, don't you want to see a bit of Garamba?"

Her eyes lit up. "Oh, yes! Show me around, Simba."

"Actually," Scar said. "Why not have Simba's new friends show you around?"

"His friends?"

"This is, after all, their home. And, meanwhile, my nephew and I can have a nice chat."

Scar noticed Simba's shoulders stiffen.

Yes. He had him exactly where he wanted him. Panicked and afraid.

"That's okay with you, isn't it, Simba?" Scar asked.

"Uh… yeah, Uncle Scar," he said, his eyes darting between Nala and the others.

"But, Simba, we've barely had a chance to talk," Nala said. "It's been six months since I've seen you. I have so much to tell you."

"You will have a lifetime to catch up now that we've found Simba," Scar said. "And I'm sure he has *so* much to tell you."

Simba's gaze immediately dropped to the ground.

Oh, yes. He was terrified of what Scar would bring up. This would be easier than he'd first thought.

CHAPTER THIRTY

Excited. Confused. Relieved. Joyous.

Nala couldn't find the right word for what she was feeling right now.

Shocked. *Shocked* was a good one.

Seeing Simba in the flesh, healthy and alive, seemed to have triggered every emotion she had ever experienced, setting them into motion within her all at once. Her mind kept going back to the moment when she had turned around and set her eyes on him for the first time in six months. This friend who she thought was gone forever, right here in front of her.

Well, he wasn't right here just now. He was back at the grotto with Scar, which was where *she* wanted to be.

After being away from him for so long, it was difficult to leave Simba's side for even a minute. Nala figured that was why she was having such a hard time focusing on the breath-taking beauty surrounding her.

It felt as if she had been waiting her whole life to see this place; she needed to take advantage of this opportunity before they set out on the journey home. As she passed through a draping moss that hung from large trees, her breath caught. It truly was paradise, its lush valleys and overflowing rivers as different from the parched land surrounding Pride Rock as one could get.

Timon and Pumbaa pointed out different spots along their walk that related to Simba in some way: The log where he'd fallen and bumped his head. His favourite tree to sleep under.

Nala had a hard time processing it all. He had started a new life here without her and his pride, and based on what she could gather from his new friends, it didn't seem as if Simba had been making plans to leave anytime soon.

New emotions began to emerge: hurt, bewilderment and just a touch of anger. They had always hoped to come here together; had he really been prepared to disregard their friendship, to leave her at Pride Rock waiting and wondering?

Timon picked a plump worm from the bark of a

downed tree and popped it into his mouth.

"Yeah, the kid was a mess when he first came here," he said around his noisy chewing. "But I told Pumbaa that we couldn't just leave him to his own devices, you know what I mean?"

"Uh, sure," Nala said. "Actually, no, I don't," she corrected. "What do you mean when you say he was a mess? Was he sick?"

"I guess you can say that," Timon said. "He was sick with worry about something terrible that happened just before he came here, but I could never get the kid to talk about it. So, I told him to put the past behind him and move on."

Something terrible that happened…

Nala wondered if Simba had seen what happened to his father after all. Witnessing such a horrible event would be devastating for anyone, but especially for Simba, who had been so close to their king.

But it still didn't explain why he hadn't returned to Pride Rock.

She wouldn't get any answers walking around with Timon and Pumbaa. She wanted to get back to Simba.

"Maybe we should go back to the grotto," Nala said.

"What? We haven't even seen the big waterfall yet," Timon said. "Now, that's the kid's favourite place in the entire forest. He floats on his back like a fish. Come on, we'll show ya!"

It would be rude to leave them, and Scar *had* asked for some alone time with Simba. She could only imagine the emotions Scar was experiencing, discovering that the nephew he'd thought had died with his brother was actually alive. They deserved a few minutes to catch up.

But Nala didn't care. She had put too much into this quest to find her best friend. She would give Scar and Simba space on their return journey to Pride Rock.

Nala glanced over at her guides.

Timon was rambling on about the time Simba had rolled into an ant pile, with Pumbaa blithely adding commentary. Zazu had joined them. He continued to pepper them with questions about the weather, the predator-to-prey ratio and other stuff she wasn't interested in.

She was betting that they were all too distracted to notice her slipping away. She slowed her pace, then stopped walking altogether. None of them seemed to notice she was no longer travelling alongside them.

Nala turned and quickly backtracked, making her way to the grotto. She had not yet turned the corner of the slick stone wall that led to the sea cave, but she could hear Scar speaking to Simba.

"I know this is difficult to hear, but Pride Rock has

truly thrived under my leadership, Simba. The lions and hyenas live together in perfect harmony. There's more food than we can eat."

What?

Nala was certain she had heard wrong. The current state of Pride Rock was the opposite of what he was describing to Simba. She rounded the stone wall and found the two huddled together, with Scar's left front leg draped over Simba's shoulders.

"If you were to return, not only would it break your mother's heart to learn what you did to Mufasa, but it would not be good for the pride," Scar said.

Nala was about to speak when she saw Scar reaching for a rock with his hind leg. He scooted it towards his front paw.

Everything started to click into place. She recalled how Scar's interest in coming to Garamba had grown when he'd learnt of Rafiki's vision, and how he had lashed out at Zazu when the bird mentioned going back to Pride Rock to inform Sarabi once Nala had told them about her and Simba's plans to visit.

She'd wondered why Scar wouldn't want Sarabi to know about Simba…

Nala suddenly realised what was happening.

"Simba, watch out!" Nala screamed just as Scar lifted the rock.

Her scream must have shocked them both because Simba and Scar both turned at her call.

Nala saw the moment Simba noticed the rock in his uncle's paw. He froze, his eyes bulging. But then he ran, scrambling on the slick rock bed surrounding the cave. Scar took off after him, his face wearing a look of pure evil.

For a few seconds, Nala was too shocked to move. Scar had just tried to kill Simba right in front of her very eyes.

He was *still* trying. The two darted past her, charging towards the area from where she had just returned.

Nala's heart jumped into her throat; the terror of everything that was happening threatened to overwhelm her. But she didn't have time to be scared. She had just found her friend again; she wasn't about to lose him.

"Zazu! Timon! Pumbaa!"

She sprinted after Scar and Simba, yelling for the others to join her. She found Simba and Scar engaged in an uneven battle. Simba tried to hold Scar off, but his uncle was more than twice his size. He was quickly overpowering Simba.

"No!" Nala screamed when Scar pinned Simba to a tree by his neck. Simba's short legs kicked chaotically, but it was obvious that he was losing the ability to breathe.

"What's going on here?" Timon asked.

Nala turned to them and nearly collapsed in relief. But

this was no time for collapsing. This was the time to fight.

"Come on," she screamed, and charged after Scar.

Nala attacked with everything she had within her, sinking her claws into Scar's back and biting so hard on his shoulder that she felt her teeth pierce his skin. He loosed his hold on Simba, dropping him, then he reared back, releasing an awful roar. He twisted and turned, trying to shake her.

Nala heard the patter of hooves pounding the dirt seconds before Scar thrust forwards and howled. She took a moment to glance over her shoulder and saw Pumbaa backing up, only to ram Scar again with his pointy tusks. Timon had clamped on to his right leg and Simba had his left; both were tearing into him.

Zazu had landed on Scar's head and was pecking it with his beak so hard that Nala could hear him hitting bone. She continued her attack, scratching at his flesh, tearing his skin with her teeth. She used the techniques Abena had taught her to hunt her most unexpected prey: the leader of their pride.

Make that the *former* leader.

The rightful leader of their pride was currently taking a piece out of Scar's leg.

They were unrelenting in their assault, keeping it going until Scar went limp.

"Is he dead?" Simba asked.

"I don't think so," Nala said. She looked over at her best friend. "We're not like him. We don't have to kill him."

"But we need to get away from him," Zazu said.

He was right.

"Come on," Nala said. And they all took off running.

CHAPTER THIRTY-ONE

This wasn't exactly how Nala had pictured seeing Garamba back when she and Simba had made those long-ago plans to visit. She only caught glimpses of the rest of the beautiful landscape as they sprinted through the dense jungle at top speed, determined to put as much distance between themselves and Scar as they could.

They had left him in a bad state. Nala wouldn't be surprised if Scar could not walk for at least a day or two. But they could leave nothing to chance. She had seen more bizarre things happen, and she knew first-paw how shrewd Scar could be. Battered and broken, he could still figure out a way to get to them.

They ran until they reached the less dense area of the

forest, the place that established Garamba's border. It wasn't until then that she finally felt safe enough to slow down.

"I think we can stop for a minute," Nala puffed between deep breaths. "Scar was too injured to make it very far."

"I believe you are right, Miss Nala," Zazu said. "Whew, these wings have got quite a workout today. I still cannot believe what just happened with Sire... Scar," Zazu amended. "What could have come over him?"

Nala had a theory about that.

"He wanted to keep power," she said.

It was so obvious. It was why he had decided they should continue their journey to Garamba instead of demanding they return to Pride Rock when he'd found her. And she had been clueless. She'd thought Scar was on her side. Yet, this entire time...

"I feel like such a fool," Nala said. "I led him right to you. I'm so sorry, Simba."

He covered her right paw with his own. "It's okay, Nala."

"I'm sorry I led Scar to you, but I'm not sorry I came," she continued. "Because you're here. You're really here, Simba."

She threw her forelegs around him in a fierce embrace. It felt as if it was finally sinking in that she had Simba back.

"Okay, okay, can we break up the lovefest? It's giving

me indigestion," Timon said. The skinny meerkat plopped his paws on his hips. "So, what do we do now that we've left the ugly one back at the grotto?"

"I say we have a look around," Pumbaa suggested. "I haven't been this far outside of the jungle in a long time."

"None of us have," Timon said. He frowned. "Just look at it. Who would want to come here?"

Nala glanced around. The leaves on the sparsely populated trees were not as green, and there wasn't a waterfall to be seen.

"It's not as beautiful as Garamba, but what is?" Nala asked.

She looked up at the sky. The sun hadn't set yet and there were a few clouds, but Nala realised that she didn't need to rely on the stars to guide them back to Pride Rock. She felt confident that between her and Zazu, they could figure out the way home.

She looked to Timon and Pumbaa. "You two need to decide if you're coming with us, because we'll need to get going. Scar may be down, but he isn't out. I don't trust sticking around for much longer."

Timon hooked a thumb at her. "What's she talking 'bout?" he asked Pumbaa. "Going where? And who is *us*?"

Nala became more antsy the longer they stood there. She knew there was no possible way that Scar was strong enough to get through the jungle right then, but she would not rest easy until she had put much more distance between them.

"We can't stay here," Nala said. "It's time for us to start our journey back home." She looked to Zazu. "You know the way, right?"

"Yes, I do, Miss Nala."

"Good." She nodded and then to Simba she said, "Let's go."

She'd already started walking when she heard, "I can't."

Nala stopped and turned. She tilted her head to the side and stared at Simba in confusion. "What do you mean 'you can't'?" Nala asked. "We need to get going. If we leave now, we can be back at Pride Rock in less than two days."

Simba took a step back. "I can't come with you."

Nala's head reared back as if he'd slapped her with an open paw. "What? Why not?"

Simba dropped his head; his shoulders slumped. "I just… I can't."

"Simba, I came here for you! Do you know what I've been through? What the entire pride has been through?"

"The pride will be better off without me," he said.

"Why would you even think such a thing?" she asked, but then she remembered where she'd heard something similar: it was from Scar before he'd attempted to kill Simba.

"Don't believe what Scar told you about life back at Pride

Rock. It was all lies. Life has been awful there, Simba." He looked up at her, his eyes widening in shock. Nala went on. "The hyenas raid the food. The lionesses can barely keep up with how much they eat. They deplete everything and leave us with nothing. And your mother—"

"No," he said. He shook his head and turned away. "Please, I can't hear any more."

"You *will* listen to me," Nala said. She had come too far and withstood too much to have him disregard her.

"You don't understand, Nala! I can't go back to Pride Rock!"

"Why not?"

"Because it was my fault!" Simba yelled. He dropped his head again and shook it. In a soft, broken voice, he whispered, "It was my fault."

Nala walked up to him. She nudged him with her nose, encouraging him to look up.

"What are you talking about, Simba? What was your fault?"

When he finally lifted his eyes to meet her, the guilt and fear staring back at her stole her breath.

"That my dad died," he answered.

Nala froze.

She couldn't possibly have heard him correctly. "A stampede killed King Mufasa," Nala said.

"I'm the reason he was there," Simba said. "If I had not been down in the gorge, he never would have gone there. He wouldn't have been trampled by those wildebeests. It was my fault."

"Simba," Nala whispered. The emotion welling in her throat made it difficult to speak. "Is this really the reason you've stayed away all this time?"

Like a bolt of lightning striking her from the sky, it occurred to her that she had been carrying the same guilt. She had blamed herself for not going with Simba that day. Nala didn't realise just how foolish it was until she heard the same coming from Simba.

"That wasn't your fault," she told him.

"But Scar said—"

"He told you lies!" Nala said.

"He told me that everyone would blame me for it," Simba said. "He told me to run away and never return, that it was the only thing I could do. I can't go back, Nala."

The compassion Nala had felt for Simba quickly turned to anger towards him. He was choosing to allow Scar and his lies to dictate his life, and she simply would not have it.

"No one at Pride Rock will blame you for Mufasa's death," Nala said. "Your mother loves you and your pride *needs* you. If you refuse to return with me, no one will believe it's because of what Scar told you; they will believe it's because you're a coward!"

He jerked his head up. "I'm not a coward," he said.

"Prove it!" Nala taunted. She stepped up to him until she was only inches from his face. "I left my home and defied my mother. I battled thunderstorms, was kidnapped by violent monkeys and was nearly killed by a rival pride of lions. I did all that without knowing if you were even alive. It was just a hunch, but that was all I needed. I was willing to do anything to bring you back home where you belong. What are *you* willing to do, Simba?"

Please. Please. Please, Nala silently pleaded.

She thought the word over and over again, but she refused to say it. She would not beg him again. As painful as it would be after everything she'd gone through to get here, if Simba decided to stay in Garamba, then she would leave him here.

"What are you going to do?" Nala asked one last time.

Several lengthy, uncomfortably silent moments stretched between them. Then that slow grin Nala had not seen in six long months stretched across her best friend's face.

"I'm going home," he said.

Nala went weak with relief, and then she jumped in the air. "Finally!"

"Well, Pumbaa, I guess we're going to Pride Rock. Wherever that is," Timon said.

"Right we are!" Zazu said. "And not a moment too soon."

CHAPTER THIRTY-TWO

Sarabi had waited as long as she could, but she could no longer hold off on making this decision. Scar, Nala and Zazu should be back by now, even if they had continued to Garamba.

As promised, Sarabi had assembled a search party when Scar and the others hadn't returned along with the new moon. But just as the lionesses were preparing to leave, a family of zebras that had stopped for rest at the water hole while on their way to the Pemba Forest reported seeing a cub and red-billed hornbill near Mount Kei. Sarabi had figured if Nala was with Zazu, it meant Scar had indeed found her.

She'd wondered why Scar would continue in the

opposite direction of Pride Rock instead of returning home with Nala, but she did not want the other lionesses to witness her questioning their leader. All that mattered was that they were safe. She had called off the search.

But that was two days ago, which meant Nala had now been away from home for six days. Scar wasn't the most empathetic leader, but he had to know that keeping Sarafina and her cub apart for this long was unacceptable. The fact that he had not returned with Nala could only mean one thing: they were both hurt. Or worse.

She closed her eyes and silently spoke to Mufasa, asking her soulmate to infuse her with the wisdom and strength he once employed as leader of this pride. She knew what she needed to do. She just had to make the decision to do it.

The other lionesses were spread around Pride Rock – most in the sleeping quarters, but others patrolling the perimeter and keeping watch over the eland that was procured last night. It was time for her to gather them together so that she could dispatch a search party out into the jungle.

Sarabi slowly made her way from deep in the cave where she had been sequestered. She kept her eyes straight ahead as she passed the lionesses and cubs restlessly hovering about the sleeping quarters. She could feel the others following her out onto the landing. By the time she turned around, all but the lionesses who were out patrolling were with her.

Expectation hummed in the air.

"I told you all that I would come to a decision if Scar and Nala had not returned by now." She sucked in a deep breath and slowly released it. "I have decided that we—"

Just then, something caught her attention out of the corner of her eye. Sarabi turned and squinted, trying to decide if what she was seeing was real or just a figment of her imagination. Four figures were running towards the clearing from the direction of the water hole.

It couldn't be…

"Simba?" Sarabi whispered.

She pushed through the circle of lionesses and sprinted down the side of Pride Rock. Sarabi ran so fast that her lungs burned within her chest. She ran with everything she had within her.

By the time she reached the figures, she could barely breathe. But Sarabi couldn't tell if it was from exertion or the stunning sight before her.

"Simba?"

Was it really him?

"Mama!"

It *was*! *It was Simba!*

Her boy was alive! And he was here!

"Oh, Simba!" Sarabi cried. She wrapped her son in a powerful embrace and wondered how she would ever be able to let go. "Oh, Simba. You're alive. You're alive!"

She registered the other lionesses gathering around them, shock and jubilance mixing in a joyful reunion. She looked up long enough to see Sarafina capturing Nala in the same embrace that Sarabi gave her own cub.

Unwilling to let him go, Sarabi reared back just enough to look down at her son.

"Simba, where? How?" She didn't even know what she wanted to ask first.

But before she could ask anything, her son disengaged from her embrace and took several steps back. Sarabi instantly felt the loss. "Simba, what are you doing? Come back here."

"Not yet," he said. "Mother, I have to tell you something."

Her heart skipped a beat. "Whatever it is, it can wait," Sarabi said. She needed to hold him, to make sure he was really here.

"It can't wait," Simba said. In a louder voice he said, "The entire pride needs to hear this."

"Simba, I already told you—" Nala said, but he cut her off.

"No, Nala. I have to do this."

An uneasy sensation quivered in the pit of Sarabi's

stomach. There was nothing more important than holding her son, but whatever Simba had to tell her, it seemed serious. At least to him.

"Mother, it was my fault that we lost father," he stated. "I am the reason he went down into the gorge. I knew better than to venture there, but Scar…" He paused. Sarabi studied him as his brow furrowed. Then, after several moments, his eyes widened. "Scar," he said again.

"What about Scar?" Sarabi asked.

Understanding dawned in Simba's eyes. Slowly, he said, "Scar told me to go down to the gorge. *He* did this. He must have planned it all along. He sent me to the gorge that day. The next thing I knew, the stampede started, and then father came from out of nowhere to rescue me. He was swept up by the wildebeests."

Sarabi's blood ran cold. Mufasa's own brother was the one who had plotted against him. He had killed her mate and had tried to kill her son.

"Where is he?" Sarabi gritted through clenched teeth.

"We don't have to worry about Scar anymore," Nala said.

"Nala, did you…" Sarafina asked.

Nala shook her head. "We didn't kill him, but he did try to kill Simba."

Sarabi listened in escalating horror as Nala recounted their harrowing battle against Scar. Her gratitude towards

Nala, Zazu and Simba's new friends, Timon and Pumbaa, could only be matched by the rage she felt towards Scar.

"We don't have to worry about Scar anymore," Nala said. "Even if another predator did not attack him before he healed from his injuries, I don't think he would return to Pride Rock."

"Not when he learns that you all have returned. He will know then that he has been exposed as a murderer," Sarabi said. She walked up to Simba and cradled his jaw in her paw. "You have nothing to explain or confess to anyone in this pride, Simba. But even if Scar had not been the one behind your father's… accident," she said, "it was no reason for you to leave."

"Scar told me I had to. He said that you would… that everyone would…" Simba choked on the words.

"Enough." Sarabi gathered him into an embrace again.

She hoped her murderous brother-in-law was not foolish enough to show his face here again. If he did, she would take great pleasure in tearing his body apart, limb by limb.

Sarabi stared into his eyes. "There is nothing you can do that I would not forgive. This is your home, Simba. You are always welcome here."

Sarabi heard someone clearing their throat just behind her. She turned to find Kito, Sefu, Fayola, Thandi and the others standing side by side. Her sister spoke up.

"If you don't mind, dear sister, the members of this pride would like to salute our king," Kito said.

As one, the lionesses and their cubs all bowed before them. Then, one by one, they took turns welcoming Simba back into the pride.

"Look who's back! Never thought we'd see you again."

Sarabi whipped around. It was the leader of the hyena pack, the one they called Shenzi.

"Yeah," the other, Banzai, said. "I was sure you would be dead within a day after we chased you off the Pride Lands."

Thandi ran up to him and tackled him to the ground. She pinned him down with both paws and bared her teeth.

"Not yet, Thandi," Sarabi ordered. Truth be told, she didn't care what Thandi did to the hyenas, but she wanted to confirm something before the lioness unleashed her destruction on them.

She walked up to the mangy dogs. "*You* ran my son away from his home?" Sarabi asked.

Shenzi held up her paws. "We were only following Scar's orders. He wanted us to kill him, but we just ran him off instead. So, you see, if it weren't for us, the little fur ball would be dead. We saved him."

A collective growl emerged from the lionesses, but Sarabi held up her paw, staving off their attack. She'd wanted the hyena to confirm that Scar was the one behind this, and Shenzi had. For that, she would spare their lives. But that was as far as her generosity stretched.

"Leave," Sarabi told the hyenas. "I want you and the rest of your kind gone from this land. And never, ever return."

CHAPTER THIRTY-THREE

The celebration honouring Simba's return had lasted well into the night. Sarabi had formally welcomed Timon and Pumbaa into the pride, pledging lifelong protection and special treatment by the lionesses for them both. Timon had immediately taken advantage of his new status, requesting that Sefu accompany him to the nearest fallen tree so that he could feast on bugs.

Sarabi had also issued an order freeing Zazu from his duties as majordomo, which Zazu had promptly declined, declaring that it would be his honour to sit at the side of Mufasa's son. The entire pride had bowed before Zazu, thanking him for his years of service.

Despite the cheery atmosphere, Nala knew the joyful

mood suffusing the air was only temporary. At least for her. Simba's return marked a new beginning for their pride, but there was still much that would have to be discussed between her and her mother before they could embark on their own journey of healing.

Nala decided that she would rather face this conversation tonight than put it off any longer. She approached her mother, who sat with several of the other lionesses cheerfully discussing what they saw for the pride's future now that their true leader had returned.

"Mother, can I speak to you?" Nala asked.

Sarafina looked at her with a smile. "Of course, Nala," she said. She gathered Nala in another hug. "Have I mentioned how proud I am of you?"

"Yes," Nala said. She couldn't deny how good it felt to hear her mother say those words. But Nala also knew they could not just pretend that the last six months had never happened.

Nala waited until they were out of earshot of the rest of the lionesses before she began.

"Mother, I know it was wrong to run away as I did," she said.

"Yes, it was wrong. But you brought Simba back to us," Sarafina told her.

"I know. But what if I hadn't?" Nala asked. "We're all

overjoyed that Simba has returned, but it doesn't change what happened between *us*. You thought you were protecting me, but all you did was hurt my chances of survival in the future," Nala pointed out.

Now that she had started, she couldn't stop. All the anger over how her mother had treated her began to pour out.

"Do you realise what you have done?" Nala continued, her voice rising with each word. "I am so far behind where the other cubs are in their lessons that it will take twice as much work for me to catch up with them. If not for Abena teaching me how to hunt, I would have starved out there, Mother! A cub younger than I am had to teach me to hunt! Not only is that embarrassing, but it could have been deadly. This can't go on!"

"I know," her mother said in a quiet voice.

Nala jerked back, unsure if she had heard her correctly. "What was that?" she asked.

"I said I know," Sarafina repeated. "I know and I am sorry." She shook her head. "I was so afraid, Nala. I was just…" She looked up at her, her eyes filled with tears. "I was so afraid of losing you. I saw what Sarabi had gone through after losing Simba and I just… I could not stand to face the same thing." She walked up to Nala. "But I should not have placed my own fears above your needs. It was selfish."

A lump of emotion caught in Nala's throat.

"I've been selfish too," Nala said.

"No. You have been wonderful," her mother told her.

Nala was the one to shake her head this time. "I should have told you and Sarabi about Garamba from the very beginning," she said. "Not just when the dwarf mongoose reported this latest sighting, but six months ago, when Simba's body wasn't recovered with Mufasa's and the talk of him possibly surviving the stampede first started.

"There is no excuse for me to have kept quiet about it, especially after the mongoose shared Rafiki's vision. Simba didn't need me out there trying to play the hero. He needed the entire pride out looking for him. We could have found him a lot sooner."

"None of that matters anymore," Sarafina said. "All that matters is that you are both here and you're both safe."

"Are you sure that's all that matters?" Nala asked. She gestured to where Sarabi and Simba still sat. The two were inseparable, even though Nala could tell that Simba wanted to hang out with the other cubs.

Sarafina dipped her head, then slowly walked towards where the mother and son sat. Nala followed closely behind her.

Sarabi spotted them when they were still several yards away. She sat up straighter, but she did not remove her front paw from where it rested atop Simba's head.

The two lionesses stared at each other, best friends who had shared both laughter and tears.

"I owe you an apology," Sarafina started.

"Sa—"

"Sarabi, no," her mother said, cutting off the other lioness. "I need to say this. What I did to you – the words I said about you – were unconscionable and unforgivable. But I hope that you *can* one day find it in your heart to forgive me."

She broke away from Simba for the first time since he had returned and gathered Sarafina in a hug.

"I already have," Sarabi said. "When it comes to something done out of the love a mother has for her cub, anything can be forgiven."

EPILOGUE

Nala looked around the sleeping quarters, searching every nook and crevice. She had been to the water hole where the other cubs had gathered, and had looked around the clearing, but had not seen Simba anywhere.

If he had run away after everything she had gone through to find him, she was going to find him again and strangle him.

Nala stopped short. A smile blossomed on her face. She knew exactly where to find him.

She raced out of the cave and up to Pride Rock's second landing. Her smile broadened when she rounded the boulder and caught sight of Simba sitting near the ledge, looking out over the vast land spread out before him.

Emotion welled in her chest at the familiarity of it all. How many times had they sat in this very spot, making plans?

Nala approached as quietly as possible.

"You're not thinking of running off again, are you?" she asked.

Simba jumped and turned. He smiled. "Never again," he said, then patted the rock next to him. "Come over here. It's been a long time since we sat up here together."

"Yes, it has," Nala said, taking the seat next to him. "You left the water hole before the leopard showed up, didn't you?"

"What leopard?"

"She is one of your mother's scouts. Sarabi had animals around the savanna and beyond searching for word about you. The leopard brought word back about Scar."

Simba's spine straightened.

"She said members of the Hatari pride arrived in Garamba and made off with him."

"Do you think they will kill him?" Simba asked.

"I don't think we have to worry about Scar anymore," Nala said.

"I guess I should feel bad. He was my uncle, after all."

"Don't," she said. "He tried to *kill* you, Simba. He killed your father. He may not have done it with his own paws, but he caused his death all the same. Don't ever think about Scar again."

After a moment, Simba nodded. "You're right. I won't think about Scar ever again."

"Focus on what's ahead of you," Nala said, gesturing at the land that stretched before them. "You know, I would sit here when I wanted to feel close to you. I wasn't sure we would ever do this again." She nudged him with her shoulder. "It's good to have you home."

"Thank you for reminding me that I have a home here," Simba said. He nodded towards the horizon, where the sun had just started to set over the Shadowlands. "Remember how we used to talk about exploring all those lands?"

"I do," Nala said. "And *you did*."

"It sounds as if you did, too," Simba pointed out. "I always said you were the bravest cub at Pride Rock."

"You did not."

"I may not have said it, but I thought it," Simba said. "Well, second bravest," he amended. "We both know that *I'm* the bravest. I mean, I was able to survive out there in the big bad jungle all on my own."

"Yeah, with Timon and Pumbaa there to help you," she said.

"Well, yeah, I guess you're right," he said.

They both looked at each other and laughed. But then,

after a moment, Simba sobered.

"As much as I enjoyed living in Garamba, I really missed Pride Rock. And I missed you, Nala. You are my very best friend. If anyone would be brave enough to face down violent monkeys and rival prides, I'm not surprised it was you."

"It would take more than monkeys and lions to keep me from you," Nala said. She looked to Simba. "Were you scared?"

He nodded. "But, like you said, Timon and Pumbaa found me and they helped me feel not so alone. They reminded me how important family really is. Not that I didn't know it before, but being away from everyone for so long and thinking that I would never be able to come back made me realise just how important everyone here at Pride Rock is to me. This is a special place."

"It's home," Nala said. "And you never have to leave again." She gestured to the land surrounding them. "This is all yours, Simba. This is your birthright. And I know Pride Rock is going to be better because you're here to lead it."